Conclave of the Cryptic 7

Volume I

Klaire D. Roy

Translated from the original French version by
James Rae

Printed and bound in Canada — Republished in February 2007 by Transcontinental.

©*Conclave of the Cryptic 7*, Volume I — Klaire D. Roy.
ISBN: 1-896523-55-2
ISBN-13: 978-1-896523-55-2

 ©Paume de Saint-Germain Publishing, Montréal, Québec, Canada, 2007.

Division of Orange Palm and Magnificent Magus Publications Inc.©
Registration of copyright: First trimester 2007
National Library of Québec
National Library of Canada

Paume de Saint-Germain Publishing©
235 René Lévesque Boulevard East, Suite 310, Montréal, Québec, Canada H2X 1N8
Telephone: (514) 255-8700 ~ Facsimile: (514) 255-0478
E-mail: info@palmpublications.com; Web site: http://www.palmpublications.com

Graphic Design: Eric Mathieu, Lucie Robitaille
Typesetting: Louise Roy, Lise Cantin

©All rights reserved. No part of this book may be reproduced in any form without permission in writing from the author, except to quote or photocopy specific passages for the purposes of group study.

English books by Paume de Saint-Germain Publishing:

- *The Spiritual Science of Essential Yoga: Techniques of Meditation, Mantrams, and Invocations*, Volume I – Sri Adi Dadi. Compiled by Martine G. Fortier, 2004.
- *Brahman's Egg, Scriptings of the Soul in Question of Light*, Volume I – Sri Adi Dadi, 1995.

French books by Paume de Saint-Germain Publishing:

- *Le Projet des 7*, Tome 1 – Klaire D. Roy, 2007.
- *Voyage au coeur de l'âme – La Voie de la Connaissance*, Tome 2 – *De nouvelles percées de Lumière inspirées de l'enseignement de Sri Adi Dadi*, 2003.
- *La Voie... à pleine Voix* – Inspiré de l'enseignement de Sri Adi Dadi, 2002.
- *Dadi Jyoti, L'Éveil d'une Lumière Infinie* – Bhai Bibi Mataji, 2001.
- *Namaskar – Lettres à Dadi (24 avril 1994 - 26 Janvier 1999)*, Tome II – Bhai Bibi Mataji, 2001.
- *La science des asanas-mudras – techniques dhyanam, dynamiques et invocatoires*, Tome I – enseignées par Sri Adi Dadi, 2001.
- *La Voie de la Connaissance*, Tome I – *Quelques percées de Lumière inspirées de l'enseignement de Sri Adi Dadi*, 1991.
- *Foudre Divine... Parfum de Rose* – Josée D. Senécal – en réédition, 1995.
- *Namaskar à mon Guru*, Tome I – Bhai Bibi Mataji – en réédition, 1995.

Forthcoming books in French:

- *Le Projet des 7*, Tome II – Ekeena Iothe.
- *La science des asanas-mudras – techniques dhyanam, dynamiques et invocatoires*, Tome II – enseignées par Sri Adi Dadi.

Table of Contents

Chapter 1	First Contacts	1
Chapter 2	Avgaard	13
Chapter 3	Star TrE.K.	29
Chapter 4	Truth or Lies?	41
Chapter 5	Do You Believe in the Spirit?	53
Chapter 6	A Danger More Dire Than Death	67
Chapter 7	Ponder Carefully!	81
Chapter 8	Russian Dolls!	95
Chapter 9	A Mudraic Conversation	109
Chapter 10	The Guardians of the 7 Temples	121
Chapter 11	Nobody on Earth is of Terrestrial Origin!	133
Chapter 12	Our Future Lives Have Already Been Lived	145

Foreword

The content of the *Conclave of the Cryptic 7* may surprise some, or even prove shocking to spiritual purists. We must admit it, we are not alone. Exceptional beings 'cohabit' our Universe, and man's isolation draws to a close. The time has come for Knowledge to circulate freely from one world, one universe, and one galaxy to another, free of all constraints dictated by the fear of the unknown and ignorance of what seems unknowable.

This first volume incites the reader to cast off his preconceptions once and for all and breach the barrier of the inconceivable. What was once far-fetched fodder for the imagination today becomes as tangible as the pages of this book. Fiction gives way to a reality that is not in the least virtual.

Conclave of the Cryptic 7 refers to the Brotherhood constituted of Beings whose existence prevails on different planets and in various dimensions. They share the common goal of the unity of all beings. What was formerly hidden must now be revealed, in order to allow humanity to progress even more rapidly along the road of transformation.

The '*Brotherhood of 7*' has accepted to reveal their existence and confide in us, at least in part, the foundations of their intercession. The Conclave's members have been assisted in their work by beings living in various worlds and spheres of activity. As participants, we are an integral part of this group.

You are invited to become acquainted with these authentic individuals, who at first glance may seem extraordinary, though further contact proves the contrary. Avgaard will surely surprise you, whereas his faithful companion Ergozs will likely incite a smile.

This book opens the door to a future waiting impatiently on mankind's doorstep for the moment to become. The concept of time and space falls away, leaving a reality in its wake that is every bit as rich as that conceived in *Star Wars* or *Star Trek*. Don't we often say that truth, or reality, is stranger than fiction? The following pages demonstrate this fact with stunning clarity: it is up to you to judge their truth...

1

First Contacts

As evening waned into night on that November 29, 2000, nothing hinted of the advent about to occur, a meeting which was to alter the course of my existence forever. Evidently oblivious of this in passing, the previous day remained a memory shrouded in its most customary attire. And as this particular Wednesday ebbed tranquilly into Thursday, I recalled only a routine sense of weariness brought on by long hours of work. Wrapped in my meditation shawl, I paused for a brief moment of meditative respite before yielding to sleep in the arms of Morpheus.

All was calm. By now, sleep had overtaken the rest of the house, neglecting to visit my room in its passage. Meditating, I revelled in this palpable silence. Stripped of my personality for a brief instant, I teetered between states, prepared to tumble into that other world to seek out my true essence.

That minute instant, the one which heralds the magical moment when surrender overtakes the self, always sparkles for me with an immense joy. I have yet to find the words to describe this precious moment to myself. It insinuates itself in me through its gentle subterfuge, preparing me to become the receptacle for the energy transmitted through meditation.

Conclave of the Cryptic

My eyelids flickered with heaviness and my spirit fell into step with the quieting rhythm of my breathing. I was just on the point of tumbling into that parallel universe… when I saw it! Its head was as round as a bowling ball. Its dark, almond-shaped eyes were immense, and its mouth was completely concealed with a gigantic collar. In fact, did it even have a mouth?

It stood before me, as real as the cushion I sat upon, staring at me as if I were some strange beast. But which of us was the stranger of the two? I couldn't quite bring myself to find it, or him perhaps, attractive, which was no doubt mutual. He was as astonishing a sight to me as I seemed to be to him, yet I felt unafraid. Now wide-open, my eyes scrutinized him unrelentingly: with my slight feminine form, he was taller than I, his body transparent as was undoubtedly his spirit too, his elongated arms stretched beyond any notion of logic. A pleasant bodily scent complemented his vaguely masculine presence. How was that possible, since he had no body? All the same, he emanated a faint sweet scent, oddly exhilarating to my olfactory nerves. Even to this day, I cannot associate this scent with any other earthly aroma.

What did he want? To communicate? Merely to examine me as an earthly specimen? He could not have traveled such inter-dimensional distances out of simple curiosity. Where did he come from? What could he possibly want? Would I be able to understand him?

One thing was certain, I wasn't dreaming. And this unearthly being persisted in remaining there, in this room, his gaze fixed on me. Moment by moment, time passed, and the more it did, the more he struck me as sympathetic. His eyes conveyed an almost convivial interest in me. Where did he come from?

– Back where I come from, there is neither good nor bad. We know very little about mankind.

My heart leapt! The sounds emanating from his form were slightly nasal in tone, giving the distinct impression of someone new to using his vocal instrument, and doing so clumsily. Incredulously, I replied:

– *But, how can I believe you?*

– There is nothing to be believed, all is still becoming. I am nameless, ageless. No more than a vibration. You are my ancestor.

Surely I had heard wrong... his ancestor? That was totally inconceivable, especially as he had just said he knew very little of man! How could that be possible? Choosing to ignore my scepticism, he continued:

You are my ancestor. We are, by this very fact, related, though this is not yet outwardly apparent. It is true that never having lived in a form similar to yours, we know very little of the human condition. However, we are integral parts of the same universe, distinct components of the same Whole. Our consummate purpose is similar, even though we exist on different planes. Your destiny intersects with our own, ultimately influencing its outcome.

– *Do we prefigure as your ancestors by virtue of the fact that our vibratory rate is less refined than yours?*

– That's sort of it. We are not your direct descendants, but our world is linked to yours through this distinctive vibratory rate. You are part of us, just

> as what you call a 'cell' is a part of you. From a certain point of view, the cell itself could be seen as your ancestor, since it embodies the most infinitesimal vibration of your self without you previously having been a cell.
>
> – *Yes, at the time of my conception.*
>
> – You were not 'you' from the moment of your conception. Your conscience was not incorporated in that primary cell. That cell is not you; while by the same token, it is you. It is a mere parcel of your whole, the most basic matter of what you are composed.

Noting my apparent astonishment, he pressed on in the following manner, 'You cannot bring yourself to understand because you limit yourself solely to known concepts. Rid yourself of the security of convention.'

He was absolutely right, I cherished my security. But if I desired to learn more, I had no other choice than to dive in, right then and there.

> – *What role will you play in my future?*
>
> – That of preparing you for a contact with us. Nonetheless, I am only an intermediary between your team and ours, fulfilling the same role you will, since you are being called upon to serve as the intermediary between ourselves and your people. You will help to prepare the 'instrument' suitably so as to become a perfect receptor of information apt to assist your species in its evolution.
>
> – *Our spiritual evolution?*

- We are not spiritual.
- *But what do you mean by 'intermediary' and 'receptor'?*
- You and I are to be the intermediaries. E.K. will be the receptor. He will transmit information that will originate from a being whose vibratory rate is superior to mine.

At that moment, I saw for the very first time the being I would later learn to know as Avgaard. His oblong head was thrust into an immense collar that completely concealed his mouth. He looked like an egg perched in its cup! His gaze, while comparable to that of his compatriot, seemed more searching and his limbs were just as elongated. A similar aroma, though even a touch sweeter, enveloped his presence too.

One distinctive feature distinguished him from his companion though... a small protuberance perched near the crown of his skull. Intrigued, I couldn't tear my eyes away from the thing, which I felt certain had a specific function. I tried to ascertain its purpose. But with a vague brush of his hand he swept my mind clean, sweeping away any interest with regard to this focal point, which was fast becoming something of an obsession for me.

- *Can you tell me more?*
- It is too soon, replied my new friend, your resistance is still too strong.

Thus they disappeared, the two of them, leaving me alone in my room. Even though the clock had just now struck one, I felt wide awake, intrigued. What had just happened? What could I make of this meeting? Should I keep it a secret? Or talk to E.K. about it? I didn't know what to think. Hoping that any movement at all would help calm my overactive mental state, I managed to undertake a few cautious steps forward. I was quite sure that I hadn't gone crazy! A mellow reminder of their perfumed presence still infused the surrounding atmosphere. I tried to make sense of the tumultuous disarray my thoughts had been thrown into, even though a deluge of 'whys and wherefores' rendered any attempt at candid comprehension virtually impossible.

I sat back down, and decided to meditate again. In doing so, I hoped to retrieve even a fleeting moment of peace that might entice some coherent inner equilibrium into the restlessness of my thoughts. I let myself be guided again to that inner haven where calm and serenity reign at all times. After but a few minutes, my agitation diminished and my thoughts became clearer. I reflected on what had just occurred and decided to speak of it as soon as possible with 'The Tibetan' and E.K., my two principal guides in this present incarnation.

In my confused state, dawn yielded tremulously to the stirring rays of the sunrise . I was still in shock. My memory constantly replayed the barely hatched events, never fully allowing them to take shape. Had I been the foil of my imagination? Where indeed resided the boundary between fiction and reality? Was everything dependent upon much more than probability and possibility? Did I really and truly encounter these beings that had come from elsewhere? Was I as unreal to them as they were to me?

Hoping for a bit of consolation from T.M., during my morning meditation I sneaked in a few tentative words to him. Far from being reassured by him, he heightened instead the chaotic feeling inhabiting me, by confirming the truth of 'their' existence. He went on to say that the second being was an 'Elder' whom he knew well. It even seemed likely that this personage served as a source of inspiration to him, while writing his classic treatise on the Cosmic Energies, which was first published in 1925.

As I seemed sceptical, he proceeded to explain further: 'Information circulates and is transmitted by a process of osmosis between the different planes of consciousness. However, it can only be correctly retrieved by persons with a mature consciousness. They must have previously undergone a strict training, thereby allowing them to become effective receptors for the higher energy frequencies. It must not be forgotten that the energy transmitted within these energetic circuits quintuples with each level of consciousness attained.'

- *How many levels of consciousness are there?*
- A multitude.
- *That's impossible!*
- Only your conscious mind can render that impossible. You must open it further.
- *Are these beings extraterrestrials?*
- Yes, they are. They don't live on this planet, but they are well acquainted with it. They keep their distance though, because their vibratory rate is greatly superior to our own. They seek strong receptors of the subtle worlds in order to transmit certain information that few among us would be able to comprehend. You now think you understand, but just you wait until later. Everything will be

shielded during this transmission process in order to protect those who are weakest in Spirit.

- *I don't understand. What do you mean by 'weakest in Spirit'?*
- Don't confuse 'weak in Spirit' with 'poor in spirit'. Spirit must be cultivated to become strong. Certain concepts must first be integrated, which will prove difficult for the majority, for whom the link with Spirit is a thousand times more minuscule than a hair.

Our conversation ended there, leaving me to unravel my perplexing thoughts on my own. We are multi-dimensional beings, limited by our lack of capacity to tune in to the higher levels of energy emanating from spheres superior to our own. In the 'here and now' it is thus impossible for us to understand everything, as our energetic circuitry could not support it. To truly exploit our multi-dimensionality, we must increase our vibratory rate, which, akin to a magnet, will attract to itself the energy required for our transformation. By so doing, we may break free from the chains of our space-time continuum and dance along with vibrations that would thus carry us far beyond anything we may have imagined, even in the very best depictions found in science fiction.

Later that day, I telephoned E.K. He didn't seem the least surprised by my account, his voice even attesting to a succession of smiles gracing his lips. It seemed that these beings were very well known to him; I therefore deduced they were even old acquaintances. He informed me coolly that the first of the two was named Ergozs, and confirmed that he was indeed an intermediary between 'us' and 'them'. Ergozs's main task was to help us in establishing contact with the second personage, who although more discreet was also more powerful. He subsequently advised me to sketch their portraits and to be ready to live a great adventure in their company. A great adventure? What kind of adventure? What was he hinting at? I hung up the phone more intrigued than ever. Obviously, life was not done surprising me. Where would it lead me this time?

As evening fell, I sketched two simple portraits of my new friends. I knew these illustrations didn't do justice to their Essence, no portrait could, nonetheless their essential energy emanated through these cleanly drawn lines, revealing their vibration. I then meditated on their images. Whereupon Ergozs reappeared.

I felt no fear: how could I? Yes, he was strange, but so gentle too. Such joy surged from his presence that it acted like a balm, calming all my inner commotion. I felt him to be amiable towards me, and ready to help me if need be. I learned he was not a master, but simply seemed to be a friend pursuing his own path to transformation, a path which appeared to converge with my own. We evolved on different spheres of existence, different levels of consciousness. I was the disciple of my master; he the disciple of his master. We were, however, so allied as to be able to hear, listen to, and ultimately understand one another.

Several days later, I met E. K. at Jean-de-Brébeuf College. I slipped the envelope with the two portraits into his hands and proceeded calmly on my way, thus avoiding his reaction upon seeing its contents. I felt anxious, afraid he might burst out laughing, which was not however the case, as he set about looking for me straight away.

In discussion with friends in the hallway before the start of the lecture he was scheduled to give, I saw E.K. subtly signal to me to follow him. Upon finding a place that would be more discreet, he slid the drawings out of the envelope. He then confirmed to me that he had already made the acquaintance of these beings, adding that we should, without delay, endeavour to enter into adjacent contact with them. My legs shaking, I replied that I was ready when he was. He smiled, and turning on his heel, said 'good work'. Incredulous, I watched him stride briskly off to give his class. Did I hear right? He recognized them! How was that possible? But contact them? How…?

The bell rang to signal the start of classes, startling me out of my reverie. I entered the classroom as if nothing had changed, while every ounce of my being screamed quite the opposite. I was no longer certain of anything, even the hardness of the floor on which I trod. Everything inside of me felt hazy and nebulous. If they really exist, what then is their place in the universe? What is it that links them to us? And what about spirituality? What role might it play in this scenario?

I saw the students smiling at me and I couldn't help thinking: If you only knew… Our apparent life is so different from the reality! Had I managed to meditate this morning? I didn't know anymore. All I knew was that my vision had been utterly transformed, the vision of my life, and of everything that makes it what it is, myself included.

2

Avgaard

In mid-December I met with E.K. at our Centre in Montréal, which at the time was still located on Sherbrooke Street. With some trepidation, I listened to his explanation of what he expected of me. My assignment would be to help him foster a receptive psychic state, one that would allow him to become not merely a channel, but a receptor of higher energy frequencies. Thus, he would be able to tune in to the wavelengths emitted by beings existing on conscious planes, worlds apart from our own. These beings, more evolved than ourselves, wished to transmit important information that could accelerate our evolution on Earth.

Without hesitation, I agreed to take on this challenge and see it through. We discussed the procedure to be followed and without further ado, we got to work. I had no idea what might develop, heightening my anxiety. As a result, this first session was unsuccessful. I was going too fast or not fast enough; I either didn't manage to intervene at the right moment or I babbled nonsense that exasperated my listener. At times, my inexperience was such an embarrassment to me that I wanted to run off as fast as my legs could carry me. But then, only a few minutes later, nothing in the world could have dragged me out from the uncomfortable chair on which I sat. As usual, I preferred some degree of discomfort, as cosiness puts me to sleep. To counteract this tendency, I tend to prefer a straight-backed chair which often hurts my lower back.

Contact was not made. Even if our first attempt left something to be desired, it took on the aura of another experience entirely. I witnessed the distress that arises when two forces of varying frequency and density attempt to come together. The atoms repel one another, rendering any fusion of their respective energy fields unattainable.

I had always believed that energies fused easily when there was concurrence between a high calibre emitter and receiver. I was proved wrong. High frequency energy fields are of a speed and density that does not allow for easy penetration of their aura. The high vibratory rate creates a force field precluding all communication.

Following this first attempt, E.K. explained to me that the sessions would have to proceed very slowly, and that contact would also have to be made gradually. Since the level of existence on which Avgaard prevailed was not encumbered by either space or time, with no human qualities there to be found, he had yet to figure out a way to adapt to a physical form. This experience thus represented a daunting challenge for him too.

I never cease to be amazed by a phenomenon that occurs during our sessions: an abrupt drop in temperature. No matter what the season, the room where we welcome these visits is always chilly. This effect is also transmitted to the world outside, resulting in weather disruptions. There had never been so many storms as in those winters of 2001-2002, nor as many in the summers that followed.

This caused me some concern. Returning to my home in Victoriaville in the midst of a raging snowstorm is definitely unpleasant. The greater the session's success, the more the weather played havoc with us. The elements basically seemed to come unhinged with this new energy trying to manifest itself in our space-time continuum.

An excerpt from my journal at the time reads:

> Stormy again today. As always when we make contact. Looks like we'll be having a rough winter!

Then, several lines lower, I question T.M., who encourages us to continue with our sessions. His explanation proceeds along these lines:

> Equilibrium must be reached between both participants before deep contact can be established. The entity is trying to infuse E.K.'s brain with an energy that will allow it to use this medium as if it were its own. It does not want to simply communicate certain information through an intermediary, but to integrate itself into this vessel so that the information received will be of the purest possible quality.
>
> —*Is it limited by our language?*
>
> Yes, but it will be able to learn quickly. It will use part of E.K.'s brain during the night to learn words, their meaning and how to apply them effectively. At the beginning, the conditions you will be working with will be less than ideal. Parasites, caused by electromagnetic disturbances

arising from outside the building, will find their way into the room. We will try to find you a more suitable location.

In accepting to take on this challenge, I had no notion of the many obstacles that we were to encounter: strident noises coming from outside and disrupting effective concentration, sudden climactic changes, scheduling conflicts, constant procedural readjustments, and fatigue brought on by this powerful new energy coming down to our level... Bad luck seemed to dog our heels, as if malevolent beings were devising strategies to counteract our work. However, far from discouraging us, this increasingly obvious little game confirmed to us that we were on the right track and that we had to continue. Which is exactly what we did.

On December 20th, real contact was established for the first time. I worked with various techniques to enable E.K. to focus his energy with minimal effort in certain precise zones of his body. I felt the throat *chakra*⋏ energizing, emanating an uncommon heat. I placed my right hand in line with his third eye, watching and listening for whatever might happen. A strange vibration, accompanied by a buzzing noise, arose from this spot, amplifying precipitously with only seconds ticking by on my watch. Sitting on the edge of my chair, every muscle in my body tensed, ready to spring into action at any moment; I waited with trepidation. I could only wonder at what would happen next. My gaze remained fixed on E.K., who was concentrating all his attention on facilitating the contact. Then I saw Avgaard

---

⋏ *Chakras* are centres of energy concentration, located in the subtle body, formed by the convergence of nadis (channels) presenting the aspect of a lotus flower.

glide into position behind E.K.'s armchair. Imposing in stature, he wore a long-sleeved coat that partially hid his hands. His long, slender fingers hovered briefly and came to rest on E.K.'s shoulders. I was but an observer, though an active, eagle-eyed one ready to spring into action at the slightest hint of any threat to my master. Although I had little idea of how to intercede, I felt ready to fly into the face of any danger.

My eyes narrowed. I saw Avgaard attempting to integrate into E.K.'s body. I was ready for anything… This integration seemed to demand a great deal of effort. The room crackled with static electricity and the incessant noise coming from outside the window surely complicated the task. My eyes were riveted on the scene… Suddenly, without any warning, the entity's eyes superimposed over E.K.'s. Surprised, I jerked back in my chair, banging violently against the wooden backrest.

The eyes looking at me through E.K.'s were immense! The energy flowing from them became so intense that every square inch of my body trembled. Though profoundly impressed, I felt no fear. Two faces in one, two pairs of eyes in tandem… Their features merged, combining matter and ether. Though my eyesight was usually not the least blurry, this unfolding spectacle seemed to be. As time progressed, my eyes, much like a camera lens, gradually brought the scene into focus. The image became clearer, and as it did I felt calmer.

I tilted my right ear towards the unseen, sensing an unknown voice before I heard it:

– Ask him my name.

Moving my head slightly to hear better, I listened closely.

— Ask him my name, repeated the voice. In a wavering tone, I spoke to E.K.:

— *He wants me to ask you what his name is.*

Without batting an eyelid, he answered:

— I know. He tried, unsuccessfully, to tell me what it is about twenty seconds ago. Try to get me to talk.

I was aware of adventuring onto a slippery slope, one leading into uncharted territory. There would be no room for error, if I asked the wrong question it risked bringing the interview to an abrupt end. I took a deep breath and started with:

— *Can you tell me the first letter of your name?*

— A.

— *The second?*

— V.

— *The next one?*

— G. Avgaard.

— *Is each of these letters related to a symbol?*

— No.

— *Is that his real name?*

— He is trying to find an equivalent. His name has many 'A's in it. That indicates that he embodies Ray 1 energy.

— *Is his name related to a planet? Or to a particular system?*

- He's not saying no. He's looking into the system… It's not in our galaxy.

- *Is he from a particular galaxy?*

- He is related, but not to a galaxy. He exists on a plane related to a planet in this galaxy.

- *Do you mean ours?*

- No. However, our planet is also related to this planet.

- *Is it beyond galaxies? Without form?*

- No.

- *Since he has a form, does it mean he is restricted?*

- Not in the sense we give to the term 'restricted'. He can't quite grasp the meaning of this word. The concept is foreign to him. That which is hidden or occult for us is clearly evident to him. The projection of restrictions or limits, as we feel them with regards to time and space, does not exist in his sphere of activity. Oh, oh… a loss of energy on my left!

- *Is this loss of energy necessary? Is it part of the adjustment you have to make for you to remain linked?*

- No, it will soon level out. Avgaard is having trouble understanding that we can take the imaginary, at least what we consider as such, for reality. We believe in our own stories. For him, this loss of energy is nonexistent. However, a part of me imagines that it is real. Now, try to get him to speak directly through me. I should be simply a vehicle to enable him to express himself.

— *Very well…I'll ask questions directly to him. To help make me feel more at ease, I'll just say 'you'.*

— *Even if you don't get an answer, keep asking your questions. We have to encourage him to express himself. Consequently, I won't try to colour what he says, or to interpret what he wants to communicate to us. He wants to speak, give him the chance! Say whatever comes to mind, just ask him questions.*

— *Where you come from, do you have different sexes?*

— No.

— *So, there's only energy?*

— Yes, a qualified form of energy.

— *Can you be more specific? Are polarities, such as positive and negative, present there?*

— No.

— *Then there is no good or evil?*

— No.

— *Are there different densities? Or intensities?*

— Different intensities exist.

— *Does a particular intensity modify, in a vibratory manner, what surrounds you?*

— It would be too complex for us to respond to this question presently. We will come back to it later.

— *Does this intensity create a kind of hierarchy? Is there a link with evolution?*

— Where I come from, there is no such thing as evolution.

- *No evolution? Is evolution found only on our planet?*

- No. It concerns several systems in different galaxies. Indirectly, we are integral parts of a galaxy without, however, taking part in its evolutionary process. I would even go so far as to say that we are more like the behind the scenes supporters of this galaxy.

- *Does this behind the scenes support further the process? Are you the originators of some processes? Are you their creators?*

- The concepts of 'origin' and 'support' are meaningless to us. Be more explicit.

- *I use the term 'support' in the sense of helping. Do you help advance processes or plans?*

- We are always ready to be of assistance.

- *Are you the creators?*

- We are the substance and manifestation, the projection of an idea, thus we are both 'creators' and 'substance' simultaneously.

- *Have you always existed?*

- Yes.

- *Have you previously undergone an evolutionary process like ours?*

- No.

- *Does the concept of God mean anything to you?*

- We are our own gods. We want to end this interview now. Good-bye.

These last words left me with the impression of being jerked to a sudden stop in mid-flight on a vertiginous parachute descent, with my objective in clear sight. I would have wanted to go on and on, but the ride was over. Distraught and disappointed, I felt my body literally slump onto the chair. E.K. gradually came back to his usual self. When he looked like he was back to normal, I asked him if he felt alright.

- Yes, Avgaard mentioned that his companions identify him as his Solar Highness Avgaard-i-Nah-I. He is highly respected by his peers. We are privileged to be able to contact him. And what about you, are you okay?

- *Yes. I would have liked the conversation to have gone on a little longer, though.*

- I know. But it's not an easy task for my physical body to adapt to that energy; I feel it to be quite physically draining. During our first encounters, the conversations will probably be fairly brief. They will get longer as I gradually become accustomed to Avgaard's presence.

The next encounter took place on December 24th, on one of those pleasant winter days when the crisp air makes our cheeks tingle while filling our lungs with a sense of lightness we can only experience at that time of year. It's a sensation that always invigorates me, reminding me of how good it is to be alive. Climbing the stairs to the Centre in Montréal, I wondered if the session would prove fruitful. Would we make contact? Would Avgaard manifest for a longer period? What dimension would we venture towards? This new adventure excited me, both due to its mysterious nature and by virtue of the multitude of possibilities that seemed to be opening up to us.

E.K. was waiting for me in the *Vak Salon*, usually a sanctuary for those wishing to read or study. A penetrating silence suffused the room, giving the impression that the session would likely be productive. We briefly discussed our procedure and began without delay. Ergozs made his presence felt instantaneously, offering guidance and advice as to how best to proceed. He took up a position to my right, whispering words of encouragement into my ear. I still felt somewhat inept in my role.

Several minutes ticked by, minutes that seemed to me interminable. I had a potent impression of being perched lightly on a crystal, until I finally felt a distinct heaviness. I resisted the urge to close my eyes. The prevailing energy seemed to be drawing me into a state of deep relaxation. Then, my mental activity went into neutral.

Despite this, my eyes remained riveted on E.K., who, in a state of deep relaxation, was preparing to receive Avgaard's energy. I asked him if we were ready. Not receiving an answer, I murmured, 'Can I ask a question?'

- Wait a bit. My state is deepening. These entities are so enormous that the necessary adjustments prove very complex.

I waited, on the alert for any sign that the time might be ripe to ask my first question. I observed as Avgaard attempted to integrate into E.K.'s body, which he seemed to be able to accomplish, without however becoming fully integrated. He studied the progress of the session without seeming to really take part. I felt certain that a silent communication was underway between Avgaard and

E.K. I tuned in with my subconscious ear, concentrating all my energy on E.K., yet I was unable to divine any of their communication. I was the simple observer of a scene from which I was mostly excluded.

Finally, E.K. raised the index finger on his right hand slightly, signalling his readiness.

- *I would like you to talk to me about similitude. This request is not my own, the question comes from Ergozs.*

- *Similitude?*

- *Yes, that between you and Avgaard.*

- The configurations are difficult to define. They are in constant flux. I perceive a myriad of colours: blue, red and violet. They are somewhat reminiscent of the aurora borealis. Magnificent colours. I have the impression I'm seeing a galaxy. Everything is in constant movement. There are pulsations, and the whole scene revolves slightly. The movement is... how could I describe it?

- *Comparable to a cone shape?*

- Yes, that's it. The top is really much narrower than the bottom. I am in a neutral sphere. To effect an adequate configuration between me and Avgaard, he has to implant a mechanism, here in my forehead — E.K. showed me a spot near his hairline — the mechanism through which these beings function. Nothing comparable exists for humankind, so he has to create this apparatus artificially.

Since Ergozs had no such implant on his forehead, I asked:

– *Not all the beings of that world possess such a mechanism, do they?*

– No, only those belonging to a certain brotherhood. It appears to be important that it be implanted in me, and then activated. It's strange; Avgaard is trying to remind me of the fact that I have already experienced this before...

– *Do you have any aspects in common that connect you?*

– More than that. For some time, I lived in this civilization and stayed at one of their temples.

– *As a guest?*

– Possibly... But I think it's more likely I lived an incarnation there.

This answer hit me like a cold shower. In a split instant, my mind went absolutely blank. This emptiness gradually yielded to a tug of war between my more rational side, and its love of security, and my irrational side, which often ends up being closer to reality than I can usually allow myself to be.

I tried to refocus my concentration. I had to be quick or I would lose the thread of the conversation.

– *Could that incarnation be one of your higher selves?*

– I have no idea.

– *You don't know or you can't talk about it?*

- To say that this incarnation is one of my higher selves would be presumptuous, which is definitely inadvisable. It's not as easy as it might seem to explain such a state of being. Perhaps I am only a facet of my true being.

- *Is it possible that this experience of having lived elsewhere is one of the facets that make you what you are?*

- I couldn't say for sure, but it's highly possible.

E.K. needed to take a breather then, which I respected. The information he had been given sent him into a turmoil, and I felt I would not be able to unlock it. It was still too soon. I would have to be vigilant in order to avoid letting my pursuit of knowledge stray into simple curiosity. E.K. opened his mouth to speak:

- Ergozs is getting closer and closer to you. He appreciates our presence. Are you sure the collar you drew, the one concealing their mouths, isn't simply a disguise?

- *It's possible.*

- I feel that the lower section of their faces is composed of a different energetic substance than the upper half. This substance is as transparent as crystal, and lights glow within it. The effect is both strange and fascinating. These are truly complex beings. We'll stop our session here for today.

I looked at the time; my watch showed that the session had lasted for over an hour. I felt stiff from sitting still so long. E.K. slowly regained his usual colour, for he had blanched considerably during this encounter. He took a deep breath, and then smiled...

– *Do you feel alright?*

– Yes, somewhat stiff, but I feel fine.

We discussed our experience for a good while, exchanging our impressions. Much work still had to be done before the contacts would reach deeper levels. We agreed to meet again in January and in the meantime to concentrate our meditations on the work ahead.

I left the Centre around 3:30 pm. A storm had blown in! Gusts of wind blew flurries of snow that clung to my windshield. I had two long hours on a highway jammed with slow-moving vehicles to look forward to. I called home, warning my family that I would be arriving a bit late. We were celebrating Christmas Eve that night, and the trunk of my car was packed with presents.

I watched the drivers in the other cars moving alongside. Brightly coloured packages sat on the seats behind them. They too were on their way to celebrate Christmas. Mine was to be different though. In a few hours, in my family's company, I would have to play the role of a fun-loving participant, though I then knew that all would be very different from now on. I surprised myself wondering if Ergozs would be there to see me tearing the wrapping off of my gifts. What would he think of all that? I remember that a smile graced my lips as I passed a lime-green Volks New Beetle, and I told myself that I was incredibly lucky!

3

Star TrE.K.

In winter, Montréal dons a cloak of paradoxes. The festive atmosphere of certain quarters makes an odd contrast with the mess caused by the spreading of salt and sand on the pavement of its boulevards. Depending upon our mood, we can discover the sparkling of stars on the fresh snow of a winter's night, or the brownish slush of a mucky sidewalk tracked with the footsteps of passers-by.

I love this season! The brightness reflected by freshly fallen snow infiltrates everywhere, suddenly illuminating the morose darkness of an autumn that often seems overly long. The houses adopt their ermine cloaks, projecting a special warmth and *joie de vivre* for inquisitive onlookers. The air smells fresh, and the ethers, bursting to overflowing, imbues the panorama with its own special translucent quality.

Those were my thoughts at that end of January as I strode hurriedly along the sidewalks, late again. I quickly bounded up the stairs to the Centre, knowing E.K. would be waiting for me, wondering what might possibly have delayed me. I headed straight for the *Vak Salon* on the third floor. There he was, with his glasses perched on the tip of his nose, perusing a book on Buddhism. He looked up... and smiled.

- Are you okay?
- *Yes, so sorry I'm late.*
- No need to apologize. Time is my friend, so I don't squander a second.

I smiled back, draping my coat over the back of an armchair. He always manages to make me laugh, despite the tension that grips me before one of our sessions. We then chatted lightly about the weather report, which had not forecast any chance of a storm for that evening.

- We'll soon see if Avgaard's presence has any effect on the weather.

Perplexed, I asked him:

- *Do you really think there might be a link between these two phenomena?*
- Yes. But we'll know for sure after our session.

That prospect didn't exactly please me. I didn't like having to get around in such difficult weather conditions.

- Don't worry. From now on, I'll make the trip.

Seeing my hesitation, he added:

- The subject is closed. My mind's made up. I don't like the idea of you traveling on slippery, snow-covered roads. What's more, I love being out in stormy weather. The roads take on an air of mystery, only revealing their secrets a metre at a time. It's like a spiritual journey, don't you think?
- *That's true. Perhaps we could alternate?*
- Has anybody ever told you how stubborn you can be?

- *Yes... you!*
- Well, there you go... I was right!

He closed his book and stood up.

- If you like, we'll discuss it another time. Right now, our work awaits us, and I feel that we had better get started. Are you ready?
- *Yes.*
- Very well, then...

We quickly took our places facing one another, and the session began. E.K. rapidly slid into a deep state of introspection. I could sense that he was on his way elsewhere, leaving our space-time continuum. His body density changed, becoming more fluid and transparent. Ever watchful, I was highly attuned to every breath he took, and every slight change in his expressions. Where was he? Had he changed dimensions, or ventured into other planetary systems?

I became his bodyguard, observing the invisible so that E.K.'s body, which in such a state was vulnerable to other forces that would like to see our project aborted, would stay safe. A shadowy brotherhood opposes man's spiritual progress. It will stop at nothing to achieve its goals, willing even to destroy a physical body. Of this threat I was well aware, having seen these forces at work on more than one occasion. These entities use various tools to attain their goals, but without any doubt whatsoever, their favourite device is the etheric circuit. It is an easy matter for them to inject a substance in a *nadi*[*], which then becomes a

---
[*] *Nadis* are the subtle channels of which the etheric body is composed.

carrier of a potent poison that gradually attacks man's physical or psychic body. That was the last thing I wanted to see happen!

Out of the corner of my eye, I could see Ergozs, watchful by my side. He spoke to me continually, offering guidance and reassurance. My eyes remained glued on E.K. His breathing was altering... becoming uneven. I tried not to panic, but to simply watch and stay calm. If a danger were to present itself, I knew I was ready. I slid to the edge of my chair, wanting to touch him... but I immediately realized it would be a big mistake! I quickly drew back my arm. I knew I simply had to be patient, never once taking my eyes off him.

Ergozs scrutinized him attentively as well, appearing fascinated by what he saw. We are so different from them. Our physical reactions intrigue them. I asked E.K. the questions I had prepared, to which he rapidly responded. That calmed me somewhat.

E.K.'s bodily form underwent a curious transformation. His head became longer, as did his arms. His mouth became smaller and his ears stretched out. I backed away to observe this more clearly. What a peculiar phenomenon it was! My eyes wide, I suddenly saw his physical form move and change aspect. As if slipping into a glove, Avgaard eased into place in his host. I watched every minute detail of the spectacle unfolding before my eyes, accompanied by an odd optical effect arising from his etheric body undergoing a transformation and encroaching his physical form. It was truly fascinating! Avgaard occupied the etheric space and E.K. inhabited the physical body. Two faces were superimposed in the same space! What an unusual spectacle! I could only wonder if I would ever undergo a similar experience one day.

I didn't dare speak to him. What he was experiencing was to my view too precious to risk interrupting with the curiosity bubbling within me. All I could think was: Where is he? What does he see? What is he doing? Is he aware of my presence? Avgaard was there, but E.K. was not. Somehow of that I was sure, I could feel it. They had momentarily swapped their respective space-time dimensions. I wondered if E.K. might be somewhere in the future, or even in another dimension. Everything around me became unstable, calling into question even my own life and the perceptions I had of it.

The limitations of the material world gradually shield themselves behind solid defences, perceptual prisons from which we must escape. Will we ever be able to do so consciously? I could only wonder.

The session lasted a full hour. E.K. slowly but surely returned to his normal state. His tone was ashen and his skin as cold as ice to the touch. His expression spoke volumes, conveying intensity and power. He knew that I knew. He knew that I had seen him cloaked in a different form from what I now saw, almost back to his usual self. I fretted with impatience, eager to discuss his experience. Still I had to wait until he had completely reintegrated into his body.

Finally, I saw him smile. The transfer was almost complete. His skin adopted its normal tone and his body, its warmth. He spoke with some difficulty.

– He brought me over there.

- *What do you mean?*
- Avgaard took me out of this world.
- *How did he do that?*
- He sampled my essence and reproduced it on his conscious plane with an adjustment to sensitize me to their atmosphere. The energy gradually infused into me. At the beginning, it was tolerable. Then, little by little, it became extremely uncomfortable, even excruciating.
- *I was afraid you might pass out.*
- I absorbed as much as possible… until reaching the very limit of my resistance. If only you could have seen the beings that greeted me! That environment was familiar to me though, I have already been there. Some of them were elated to see me, others seemed simply curious. For them, I was an extra-terrestrial. They were proud to have attracted into their dimension a human prototype capable of remaining stable, on the same wavelength, without disappearing.
- *Like being teleported, or beamed up as in Star Trek?*
- Yes, that's a fair comparison. This stability encouraged them. Now they know that communication is possible. In me, they discovered a transmitter capable of helping draw their dimension and ours closer together. I act as a sort of a memory chip in their system. Despite the fact that they are devoid of emotion, they give off a great deal of warmth. In their system, love as we know it does not exist, instead taking the form of a thermal fire. A rare

goodness, something pure, emanates from their beings, and to them evil is unknown. They are higher, superior forms.

— *Can you describe the place where you found yourself to me?*

— It's hard to give an exact description. It was like an open-air temple supported by sparkling white marble columns glittering with tiny crystals.

— *Was it transparent?*

— Almost. Obviously this picture cannot truly reflect the reality of what I saw. Our minds always try to rationalize the information they receive. They turn the vibrations we perceive into images, and when these vibrations have their origins in other dimensions, some disparity results. How about you, what did you feel or see?

— *Avgaard was more present. Was that because a part of you had been taken away?*

— It's possible. With consent from my essence, he projected his power into my physical self so that his presence could inhabit it.

— *I had the impression that he felt some of your suffering.*

— True. That way he could measure the intensity of the discomfort I was experiencing.

— *Your bodily form changed, and your breathing became irregular. Ergozs was also very much in evidence; it seemed to me as if he wanted to offer reassurance. I asked him if he was a disciple of Avgaard's and he told me he wasn't a disciple, but rather an aide.*

- Where they are from, there is no such thing as a sub-class of followers. In that dimension, all citizens are free and equal. However, they recognize the vibratory superiority of certain individuals among them. They consider them as leaders and treat them with due respect.
- *I asked Ergozs if they were servants of God. He mocked me, mentioning that for them God does not exist.*
- He is right. God is the manifestation of a human concept, one we created.

The conversation then took a very interesting turn. The concept of God had always fascinated me; perhaps I would learn something that could help lift the veil of this mystery?

- While I was in their dimension, they asked me, 'Why do you need God? Have you not discovered that in yourselves?'
- *It's strange that you were speaking of God at the same time as Ergozs and I were discussing the very same thing.*
- No, it's not strange at all; it simply proves that we were linked, in close contact through different dimensions.
- *Ergozs asked me why I wondered about the existence of God. I told him it was out of simple curiosity. He then led me to understand that such idle curiosity is just a waste of time.*
- He's right. For them, that sort of questioning is totally useless. They have gone beyond the phase of dependence on a divinity. They are creators and they know that all there is issues from them.

— *What was that?*

— Everything originates from them. Thus, the invention that is God is for them a waste of time.

— *They state that God is absent from them.*

— They simply mean to say that they have been exorcised of this principle.

— *Of the concept of God?*

— Yes.

— *If, as human beings, we dispensed with this concept, what would become of us? Nothing would happen?*

E.K. smiled at that question, and pressed on.

— Not long from now, you will no longer be a mystic.

— *My concepts related to God are being shattered to pieces. I always believed in a superior power, and now, what or whom can I believe in?*

— This power exists, but it must not be personalized. The concept of God was created in our image, and not the inverse. We have limited this power, imprisoning it in matter whereas it extends far beyond. To limit God is to limit ourselves to being much less than we really are. Do you understand what I'm trying to say?

— *Yes, but it's stronger than I am! I need to qualify God, to give Him a form, even if it's somewhat diffused, or akin to some kind of light.*

— That's a natural tendency, but God is indefinite. He cannot be rationalized, nor can He be understood by our concrete mind. Attempting to arrive at a definition plunges us into the depths of the greatest mystery of all. Words cannot elucidate this mystery. He is vibration, and words are limitations. Relax and let the energy do its work. Your vision will gradually change and open up to other dimensions, the existence of which you have never even dreamt of.

E.K. studied my perplexed expression, and smiled again.

– Are you embarking on another crusade against your concepts?

– *It seems so. I have the impression I've fought quite a few battles since I met you.*

– That is part of the process. Nobody can avoid it. Did Ergozs mention anything else to you?

– *Yes, he is getting to know us, though we still appear strange to his way of seeing. He mentioned that we are fond of principles that he cannot even conceptualize.*

– You see, even he notices. Concepts are meant to evolve, they shouldn't limit us anymore. Happily, I cling to no such concepts. I am able to dispense with them at will. Nonetheless, I have deliberately chosen to retain some of them in order to remain close to you, in human terms. That way I can comprehend your torments.

– *Otherwise, we wouldn't be able to understand you, and you would seem inhuman to us. That would put a wall between us and you, wouldn't it?*

– That sums it up precisely.

E.K. eased into another smile. His physical body might have been tired, but not his spirit.

– Why don't we go get a coffee?

– *That's a wonderful idea!*

Getting to my feet, I realized I was a bit stiff. A coffee would do me a lot of good.

– You can go on down, I'll join you in five minutes.

I left the room. The hallway was unusually quiet. I felt somewhat dizzy. But what if God was only a myth? Treading softly, I made my way to the door, donning my coat on the way down the stairs, looking forward to a breath of fresh air to clear my thoughts. In the lobby, the street noise reached my ears. It was snowing... I felt relaxed. Heading for the restaurant, I found myself wondering if it would stop snowing soon. Ordering two coffees, I stood busily jotting notes in my notebook. I didn't want to forget a thing! That's when E.K. caught up with me.

– Did you look outside?

I looked up, following the direction of his gaze. The power of the rising storm out the window could be seen reflected in my face. The snow whirled, obliterating sky and ground alike. E.K. nudged me teasingly. He had won again! From then on, the sessions would be scheduled once weekly in my office... in the hopes that the weather would be more forgiving for his return journey home.

4

Truth or Lies?

With the arrival of the March lion, winter gradually withdrew to its lair. It was a particularly hard winter this year. The snow banks, heaped into mounds over dormant flowerbeds, looked like enormous vanilla ice cream cones. In hundreds of towns across Québec, their size grew to proportions that dwarfed the roofs of the houses. Such a phenomenon hadn't been seen since the 1970s.

On the road to town, my car purred like a happy, well-fed kitten. The other cars, their drivers impatient behind the wheel, were all spackled with salt stains. The winds swirled and gusted, frenetically stimulated by the conjunction of winter and the coming spring. The long period of ice and cold had worn all of us down, and we fretfully awaited the revival of spring, which by any indication would to be late in opening its first buds.

As I drove cautiously on the pavement wet with the spring thaw, I reflected on recent events. I felt privileged to have lived through such a marvellous experience. Nevertheless, I realized that a part of me still clung to false beliefs, beliefs that kept me from plunging headlong into the thick of the action, charged with setting the stage for the future.

I may have wings, as we all do, yet I often doubt their existence. Although they're sturdy, any flight entails risks, and I sometimes crash land due to the overwhelming might of certain winds. At the time, I felt like I was poised on the edge of a precipice, waiting to take the leap into the void. I wondered if I needed a push, as often proves to be necessary.

I parked my car on a street intersecting Sherbrooke, picked up my notepad and climbed out. I felt the sun's warmth on my face as I headed to the Centre with a quick stride. The hurried people I crossed paths with didn't even spare a look for those they encountered. Their drawn features betrayed an inner state guiding them to a goal that seemed to escape them. Nonetheless, despite my observations, I felt like I was walking on air.

I cheerfully climbed the stairs leading to the third floor. I was in Montréal to meet some people later that evening, and we decided to take advantage of the occasion to work before the scheduled rendezvous. I saw E.K. meditating in the Jnana Hall. Silently, I slipped into the hall and prepared to meditate as well.

At times I converse with certain masters during my meditations. Over the years, I have become used to their surprise visits. Undoubtedly, one of my greatest deceptions in spirituality has been to discover that these masters are not the least bit mystical. Of course, they are warm and full of love, but they are also direct, temperamental (yes, they sometimes get angry!) and exacting in their demands. As with any good teacher, they are always ready to explain, guide and encourage a student sincerely seeking help and assistance. And as anyone who wishes to communicate with them will find, patience and the art of lending an ear to the imperceptible are called for. Our antennas must be tuned acutely, for these beings are very discreet and absolutely respectful of our space. Those who don't know how to listen and observe will neither hear nor see any sign of them.

On that particular afternoon of a long winter drawing reluctantly to a close, nothing hinted that a master would come to meet me. I had sought no advice and in the warmth of that hall only sought one thing – silence and serenity to soothe my spirit! Drawn to that unnamed haven that welcomes me and frees me from the stress and constant inquisitiveness that assails me, I slipped into meditation and found my true self once more, that of a divine essence clad in human form.

On the screen of my closed eyelids a face took shape. The features were fine, with glowing skin, long and shiny hair, and a dark and intense expression… the Himalayan Master! His visit surprised me; it had been so long since I had seen him! My inner being marvelled at such beauty. I waited for him to become even more manifestly apparent. His complexion was perfection itself! Any woman would die for such skin tone.

H.M. watched me closely. I tried to deduce his frame of mind, impossible! His impassivity, though not detracting from his warmth, revealed nothing of his inner state. He is a mystery, and a mystery he would remain. He would never pay me a simple courtesy visit! To what did I owe this honour?

— Many masters support you in your project.

I was startled, not expecting such a frank statement. Was he talking of the 'Avgaard' project? If so, why? This project was still in its nascent stages, how could he have already been informed? Naively, I asked him:

- *Do you mean the 'Avgaard' project?*

- *You shouldn't refer to it as the 'Avgaard' project, since several others will become manifest through this one. Multitudes are watching and scrutinizing.*

I was disconcerted. Who was he alluding to? I didn't dare ask him, as impressed as I was by his very presence. I stammered clumsily:

- *We have great hopes for the success of this project.*

- *So do we, but we don't want to impose any additional stress on you. You are carrying out your task admirably. This project is a precursor to anticipated plans, advancing them by twenty to thirty years. We are thus very pleased, but not impatient.*

- *By twenty to thirty years! But why was E.K. chosen if someone else would have been suitable? Doesn't he already have his hands full with what he has set out to accomplish with us?*

I immediately regretted having spoken out of turn; I should have held my tongue. Had I dared question the good judgement of the masters? My spontaneity sometimes plays tricks on me. H.M. patiently responded to my impulsive query.

- *We could have waited, but the vehicle would have been of lesser quality. We are thus extremely pleased that such a receptacle could be made use of. The quality of the information transmitted will certainly be much higher. You are doing good work, persevere.*

Without another word, H.M. vanished, leaving me perplexed. For the umpteenth time, I felt bewildered. Where were we? I could see the weight of the task laid on E.K.'s shoulders getting heavier, expanding the range of his responsibilities. My nature rebelled. I am stubborn, and my inner questioning only serves to prove it. The whys and wherefores played leapfrog with each other in my mind.

I watched E.K., still meditating. Had he any inkling of the magnitude of the task ahead?

– Yes, he knows, responded a familiar voice.

My heart gladdened with this pleasant surprise. Two masters at the same time, it was really too much! If two of them deigned to become manifest, there was really something suspicious afoot. Was this project more important than I had suspected?

T.M.'s face appeared only centimetres from the tip of my nose. Though not quite as handsome as H.M., his voice was just as intense and resonant. I love this master, though he seldom treats me with kid gloves when he talks to me. Direct as he is, he appreciates my stubbornness when put to good use and respects me as I am, flaws and all, without quite accepting them. He stimulates me, encouraging me to transform and daring me to cast off my old frayed cloak of complexes and misconceptions.

– The time draws near for E.K. to attain his full potential. Some will recognize this as such, others will be unaware. He will take his place among the elite few with supreme knowledge of the planet. He will know and be known.

He is not alone. A team is taking shape around him, a solid, dependable team. His true friends will become apparent and his time of secluded isolation will come to an end. He should know that we support him as much over there as we do here.

At present, he is developing a project that he will soon submit to us. This project will bear fruit. He is who he is, and we will help him to become more. His period of expansion is beginning, and he will need solid, dependable support. He is no longer alone... he should know he is well-loved and appreciated by all! He is ours and one of our own. He will complete his mission both without fail or regrets. He will only return in another incarnation if he so desires, for his mission here draws to an end.

– *Will he take the Bodhisattva vows?*

– We sincerely hope so. The choice, however, is freely his to make. He belongs to the Cosmic Order, which directs him in his destiny while respecting his wishes. Wishes that are no more than mere appearances, as he is exempt from desire. He is linked to us, and we are linked to him. We love him despite these trying times he has had to endure, in hiding his true countenance from us. Sometimes he has sought to escape, but he has never disobeyed. He is one of the loyal among the loyal brotherhood that we are. Our blessing goes with him as he accomplishes his destiny.

Then T.M. paused momentarily to look upon me kindly, before concluding with these heartening words.

— Don't worry; all will be for the best.

At that, he disappeared.

E.K. was still meditating, seemingly oblivious to what had just occurred. Of course, this was only an illusion, as he always knows everything!

Thus we sat, in silence. A half-hour had just ticked by on the clock. The ambient air wafted a scent of jasmine, revealing the powerful presence of Saï Baba. He was there too, looking on from the invisible. How could a man so slight in stature be so great in nature?

E.K. smiled too, having sensed his presence. In mutual agreement, we decided that the session would take place in the Jnana Hall under the vigilant gaze of a virtual Saï Baba.

We took our places facing one another. I felt a great calm suffusing me. E.K. immersed into his inner state. Avgaard approached immediately and I saw him gradually integrate into E.K.'s bodily form. I wondered, would he be able to make himself heard?

I observed each and every one of E.K.'s slightest movements. I had to be attuned to the precise moment for verbal intervention. Too soon, Avgaard withdrew and left the receptacle. Too late, E.K. became inscrutable, his consciousness nowhere within a thousand miles of where we were. I had to seize the opportune moment, and only the invisible aspect of his presence could reveal it to me. His physical presence, which seemed inactive, would yield me no clue. My gaze fell upon one of his embodiments, and I saw it speaking to me. When the opportunity presented itself, I wanted to catch it on the fly. Looking for answers, I studied his 'KA' or etheric body; part of it was elsewhere, and the other part was in service of Avgaard's energy. Finally he initiated the sign with a slight movement of his right index finger. I waited... Minutes passed, my gaze remained fixed on that finger. At last he moved it... in the ether. He was ready to speak.

– *Can I ask you a question?*

– *Ask your question.*

– *Can you speak to us of Truth?*

E.K. smiled.

– Truth, in your view, is it objective or subjective? In your realm are there a multitude of Truths or only one sole Truth? Are some states truer than others? Can a lie contain the Truth or can the Truth be only what it is, while expressing in some manner a so-called falsehood?

Nobody can claim to have the Truth, as it belongs to no one. Is the word Truth synonymous with reality? Is there a reality, or a version of reality, in which we could say that Truth reigns supreme and supports that reality?

It is extremely difficult to approach the reality of Truth. Any conception of the Truth is no more than an approach to what is essentially inexpressible.

Truth is neither an idea nor, in reality, a reality. To be true means or seems to suggest that we are more real, more deeply who we are. In reality, there is no self. We have never belonged to ourselves, and no self belongs to us. Is that a Truth?

Truth holds in its core all that is considered false. It lends to the false, to *Maya*⁺, its apparent reality. It confers the right to be and to exist on different levels of semblance. The false, from our point of view, is neither superior nor inferior to the Truth. Sometimes it allows us, through the intrigues of Maya, to elevate to a superior evolutionary level by projecting in us certain illusions that must disappear when the level is attained.

Everything is subject to change and everything can be considered as either Truth or falsehood, depending upon the individual's outlook relative to a certain situation. Am I Truth or a Falsehood in your eyes? Only you and your particular view can answer.

E.K. abruptly ceased talking. That was how the interview ended. I drank in each word that had been uttered. Had I experienced a dream or a false illusion, I wondered? Had I encountered a Truth or an aspect of reality? I didn't know anymore, and it mattered little to me. All seemed more or less real, even my own physical form. Was I simply a projection of my true identity?

I wrenched myself out of my reverie, to concentrate my gaze once more on E.K. Avgaard was gone. E.K. slowly reverted to his normal tone and appearance. Then he smiled at me.

– Are you alright?

– *Yes, what about you, how do you feel?*

⁺ *Maya* is the energy force that makes the unreal appear real, and the ephemeral seem eternal, dissimulating our divinity.

> – I feel like I'm both here and somewhere else at the same time. I'm still having a bit of a hard time retrieving my bodily sensations. It's very demanding to abandon oneself to energy so different to our own. My body puts up a lot of resistance.

Surprised at that, I couldn't help commenting.

> – *I never would have thought you would feel such resistance.*

> – I'm still human, don't forget that. I have to outmanoeuvre certain laws due to the effects of gravitational force on the human condition.

> – *All of this is so complicated.*

> – The complexity arises from your intellect. Let your intuition do its job. By using it, your understanding will be redoubled. I'm famished! How about going out for a bite?

> – *Sure, great idea!*

> – What do you say, Japanese or Italian?

> – *Italian?*

He smiled at my eagerness, knowing I'm crazy about Italian food. Feeling elated, we donned our coats and left the Centre. The sky had clouded over, and a brisk breeze seemed determined to chill us to the bone. E.K. drew in a deep breath:

> – I smell snow coming our way!

I burst out laughing. Yes, without a doubt we would get snow. Like two old partners in crime, we set off down Sherbrooke Street on the hunt for an Italian restaurant.

– So, what are you waiting for? You're not going to tell me you met up with H.M.?

– *You know?*

– How can you have any doubt?

In the hubbub of the street, I related the details of our encounter, undaunted even by the roar of a passing tow truck. Life was as it should be. I had never felt so glad to feel my feet touching solid ground.

5

Do You Believe in the Spirit?

The days seemed to rush by at a vertiginous rate. If the date marked on the calendar was to be trusted, it was already March 13th. How was that possible? In a month, to the day, the second spiritual symposium hosted by the Canadian Ashram was to begin.

I gulped a mouthful of hot coffee and winced… it was too hot! For the past while I had been running on coffee, as the days were endless. I couldn't do without its stimulating effect.

Setting down my cup, I glanced at the hodgepodge of papers piled on my desk. I oversaw several committees charged with organizing the symposium and could see that at times one committee's mandate stepped on the toes of another's, or vice versa. This involuntary crisscrossing, though necessary, sometimes led to pointless conflicts which then required further attention to defuse. Everyone involved was doing excellent work, but fatigue and stress sometimes give rise to misunderstandings that can lead to conflicts. Vigilance and conciliation were my watchwords.

I didn't know which way to turn anymore! I had to think of every last thing, even if that last thing likes to conceal itself in the tiniest details, which, if ignored, could prove disastrous.

For example, Dannion Brinkley, one of our invited guests, is he a vegetarian? Does he want to come accompanied by his spouse? Should he be met at the airport? Does he want a smoking or non-smoking room? Will he bring copies of his books or should we make sure to have some on hand? The questions and last-minute changes dogged us all incessantly.

And Avgaard, where did he fit into all that? He too needed some of my time and energy.

I gazed out my office window, conjuring a flight of fancy. Sometimes, I wished I could be a thousand miles away. I pictured myself seated at a Paris café, revelling in an enormous bowl of *café au lait*, or in Venice enjoying a scrumptious pizza or perhaps simply sipping a glass of fine wine from the South of France. I pondered; maybe a vacation would do me some good?

I chuckled to myself. Such an easy answer was easily deflected by listening to Spirit's rejoinder, imbued with wisdom and a touch of humour. What could possibly be more exhausting than a vacation? And I already felt so weary. The time was surely not yet ripe for a vacation! Bemused, I smiled as I dialled Lucie's cell phone number. Some details of the artistic entertainment had to be seen to, and what's more, it turned out that the hall was unavailable for our final rehearsal. We needed to find a solution. I thought so hard that the wrinkles in my brain found themselves reflected in the furrow on my brow. What was to be done?

As Lucie and I discussed the ins and outs of the problem, I saw a familiar car pull into the parking lot. I then told Lucie we'd have to finish putting the pieces of the puzzle together later. The project with E.K. came first!

E.K. entered my office, looking somewhat drained. He smiled warmly at me. I relieved him of the two coffees he'd brought with him, knowing we'd scarcely have time to drink them. The symposium placed a burden on all of us, and E.K. was not immune. Did he even have time to sleep? I doubted it. The huge load he took on and saw to completion would easily have been enough to keep three men busy twenty-four hours a day. We chatted a few moments, knowing full well there was little time for idle chitchat.

Without wasting more than a few moments, we began our session. I dimmed the lights and lit a stick of incense to set the mood, and then we took our places.

I felt edgy, squirming on my chair as if a colony of ants had made it their home. This inanimate object, my usually welcoming chair, seemed to be trying to reject me with all its innate power and try as I might, I couldn't find a comfortable position. Without raising an eyebrow at my obvious agitation, E.K. advised me to try meditating for a few minutes.

– You have to relax; otherwise your mental agitation will interfere with the session we're supposed to have. I'm going to step outside for a few minutes to get some air.

– *But it's freezing out!*

– I know. Don't you think I'm old enough to figure out what's good for me or not?

I could see how silly and futile my comment had been. He was right. I had to calm down, which I should have done before he arrived. I had failed at my task and I was glad he had shown such delicate tact in pointing this out to me.

He pulled on his coat and stepped outside into the icy cold. I sat with my fingers interlaced and recited a mantra, one of the most effective means I knew of to calm my surging mental state.

I took a deep breath, fully savouring my moment of peace. Like a ship becalmed in a bay, my being let itself be rocked gently by inner silence. I yielded to the feeling, persuaded that nothing could reach me there to interrupt my peace.

– You should paint!

My heart almost jumped out of my chest. It was such a shock that I placed my hand over it to prevent it from escaping and convince it to stay right where it was. It was beating at a hundred miles an hour! My eyes wide open, I saw T.M. watching me.

– *You scared me half out of my wits!*

He couldn't help but smile at that.

– You should learn to be on guard at all times, especially when meditating. To meditate is not to go off into a cave away from everything. To meditate is to open yourself up!

I listened attentively, trying to put my ideas and my inner state back into some semblance of order. I had the distinct impression that his sudden apparition was no accident. He likes to tease me and sometimes he can't resist the impulse to pop into my space without warning. He suddenly appears like a ghost out of nowhere, amusing himself with his victim's reaction.

– I hope you don't expect me to make an appointment?

I smiled at his gentle humour.

– *Of course not.*

– The disciple is of service and must always be ready. Are you?

– *I am.*

– Good. So, I said you should paint.

– *Paint what?*

– Paint pictures of Avgaard, Ergozs...

How could I ever live up to that challenge? I was able to scribble when I had to, but to paint? I knew I would have to ask for help.

– *Are we on the right track in conducting this project?*

– Yes. You must persevere. You will write books, as the work will mainly be accomplished through the literary medium. Practice and learn to modulate your voice. It must become E.K.'s guide into the depths of his unconscious. You will help plunge him into the furthest depths and bring him back to the surface.

– *Why work in this way?*

– His mind is too powerful. He is in control and is its master in all aspects. He must now master another aspect, more in tune with his level of initiation: total abandonment of self to the immense being that inhabits him, the one we know as E.K.

– *Was Avgaard a master for E.K. at some other time?*

– No, but he is a master in his own realm. He will help E.K. to reveal himself and augment his power through the being we know in this incarnation by the name of R.F.C.

— *Aren't E.K and R.F.C. one and the same?*

— They are, but at this time their natures are separate due to ions of knowledge. The actualization of E.K. in R.F.C. will enable this knowledge to do its work of channelling the information needed to help humanity progress to its destiny.

— *Can't you accomplish that task on your own?*

— No, that is not my appointed task. The assistance I offer humanity has an impact on other planes besides the physical. E.K., through the liaisons of Dadi and R.F.C., is more involved on this plane. Possessing a physical body allows for a greater understanding of man in all his suffering.

— *Sometimes I feel that he is very tired, nearly exhausted.*

— The adjustment is not an easy one. Don't worry, he is not in danger. Get to work now.

At that very same moment, E.K., his ears and the tip of his nose ruddy with the cold, pushed my office door open. March winds can often prove quite frisky, easily affecting the exposed and more thin-skinned areas of our facial anatomy with their chill.

— So, did you meditate?

— *Yes... and T.M. dropped by for a visit.*

— What did you talk about?

As he warmed up I recounted our conversation. He listened with avid attention.

– He didn't say anything more?

– *Yes, there was one thing he mentioned just before he left.*

– So, what does this 'one thing' consist of?

I didn't want to talk to him about it yet, preferring to wait until after our session. I really didn't like to allude to the dark forces that had been doing their best to make life a living hell for the past while. Sometimes, they pile one obstacle on top of another, hoping to create chaos in and amongst us and the Ashram. We had to be constantly on our guard to evade their ploys and manoeuvres.

– *He mentioned the dark forces.*

– I know. What did he say?

"The dark forces are backing off, and a change is on the horizon. However, the effects of their efforts will still be felt for the next few months. Their attacks will be somewhat less vigorous, but they will resume in full force during that period you call 'The Festive Season'. We must remain vigilant. They haven't finished their task and are only waiting for 'the right moment', which will not arise, at least not in the way they might wish."

– *I asked him what that could mean. He elaborated:*

"Those who will fall victim to their influence are of lesser importance. Their wish is to destroy the Ashram, and they will not succeed in doing so. We will keep watch over you. The stronger ones will stay. These words are not meant to reassure you, but to serve as a warning to be on your guard. Though we are combining our efforts, we cannot accomplish the work you are doing. Our power resides in combining forces."

– *That's it, that's all he said!*

– Interesting. We will be on our guard.

Looking somewhat thoughtful, E.K. continued gently...

– Our task is a difficult one, isn't it?

– *No, on the contrary. Such opposition makes me want to work even harder.*

– That's good. Shall we begin?

– *Yes!*

E.K. took his position facing me. He seemed to me to be taller and more imposing than before. Could that be due to Avgaard's influence? He smiled faintly.

– See you soon!

His eyes closed and the session began. I articulated and modulated my voice more than I had been doing. Every frequency emanating from my mouth shaped a vibrating note that then played on E.K.'s aura. It was hard for me to hit just the right note. Too high and I could sense his energy field recoiling with irritation, too low and a release of the tension required to establish contact ensued.

Ergozs was there, close by my side, his presence a source of reassurance to me. He watched E.K. with a great deal of interest, at one point asking me:

– Is it normal for his ears to become so red?

– *Yes. He was outside, and it is very cold.*

– Does your physical body always react in such a manner?

– *Yes, our physical bodies react that way because they need a fresh blood supply to warm us, which also serves to reinvigorate his energetic circuit.*

Do You Believe in the Spirit?

- If not, what would occur?
- *Without sufficient blood circulation, tissue dies and decomposes.*
- Is that painful?
- *No, not really, only uncomfortable.*

Ergozs watched me for a few moments before continuing.

- You are very privileged to live such an experience. I would like to feel what cold is, what a touch of the skin feels like, or the feel of clothing.
- *You don't feel touch?*
- No, we feel something else.
- *What is that something else?*
- I cannot tell you. It is not my mandate to do so.

Disappointed, I looked back to E.K. and noticed that Avgaard had drawn near. He had taken up a position behind him, his hands on E.K.'s shoulders. I shuddered slightly, seeing his long thin fingers that must easily have measured fifteen centimetres. Though I didn't find them beautiful, they were definitely impressive. He looked up at me and I heard him say:

- The instrument is almost ready.

Instrument? How could he call E.K. an instrument? I tried to remain calm, as any agitation could interfere with the procedure taking place. I tried to banish the word 'instrument' from my mind and simply concentrate on E.K. and Avgaard. There was a job to be done, and I would do it. I wondered though, 'Do they, just as we do, have a soul or a Spirit?'

I altered the voice I was using to address E.K. The tone came out soft and calm, which reassured me. Avgaard gradually completed his integration. The ethers blended, rendering my visual picture of E.K.'s physical self more blurry. This effect fascinated me; the human being never ceases to amaze me!

I patiently held off until exactly the right moment for a more direct intervention. E.K.'s breathing slowed, becoming barely perceptible. His skin became luminous, glowing transparently, and his facial features merged with Avgaard's. I only wished I could have fixed that image on film!

Then Avgaard's index finger signalled.

- *Can we begin?*
- Yes.
- *Do you have a soul?*
- The soul cannot be possessed. We envelop it in its nature.
- *Do you believe in Spirit?*
- What about yourselves?
- *Yes, we do.*
- The Spirit interpenetrates all. It emanates from the Breath of That Which Is. Some call That Which Is: the One Source, God, Existence, Truth, or Consciousness. Spirit makes the impossible possible. Through its unifying principle, it gives meaning to existence. It is the true goal, the true foundation of the Consciousness through which man can express who he truly is.

For us, Spirit is not only the ether we consciously breathe in, but also our sole hope. It is the very essence of what inspires us, the principle allowing us to reflect, to see and to know.

Spirit is this constant source upon which we depend. It confirms the hope that we are at once God, angel, man, and formless form. We bless the fact that Spirit communicates a way of being to us, permitting us to know God intimately, far from the human concept of God.

Spirit is the fire that nourishes us, and this nourishment is an integral part of the fabric of the beings that we are. Whether or not we decide to assume a form, for us Spirit is fire. However, this has nothing in common with the fire that burns and purifies (you) through the process of suffering.

You hope, through this fire that consumes you, to heighten your sensibility and draw even nearer to what you already are, which is to say 'divine'. This gap between what you think you are and what you really are, is artificially created by the intercession of time, which is essentially relative, artificial and fictitious.

The fire, the *kundalini*[*], is manifest in you in a way that sometimes seems painful to you. It throws you into a mental and physical imbalance, upsetting your emotional body in its passing, blurring the vision between that which must be worked on and

---

[*] *Kundalini* is the primordial *shakti* or cosmic energy that is found lodged at the base of each individual's spinal cord.

that which must be left alone. Through this false vision, a great deal of time is lost in many attempts at changes which must not yet occur, or should have been made a long time ago. Good timing is critical, and accurate vision is equally so.

For you the kundalini is no more than a little match that suddenly catches flame because of the friction caused by suffering or due to a lived experience. A grace then ignites within you to enable you to align your inner selves, through the centres known as *chakras*, thus tapping into a greater energy source whose potential resides in all of you.

This power travels along a spiral pathway, guiding you to possibilities and potentialities related to your human experience. Thus, your genes can all evolve within a circle of existence reserved exclusively for the evolution of your species.

Only you have access to this circle which we cannot affect directly. Our link is Spirit, which interpenetrates our two worlds, occupying the space existing between you and us. Thus, you are part of us without being part of our Universe. Spirit permeates the very fabric of our dimensional being and continues to what we call the infinite, beyond our vision. We could say that Spirit is for us what Love means to you!

We now wish to conclude this interview. Be blessed!

And so the session ended. Avgaard exited the 'instrument' and left the room, followed closely by Ergozs. E.K.'s eyes opened. He looked tired, yet serene.

- *How are you doing?*
- *I'm good, what about you?*
- *I feel pretty good too. Do you know what term Avgaard used to refer to you?*
- *No...*
- *He called you the 'instrument'.*

E.K. burst out laughing.

- *That's exactly what I am.*
- *But don't you find it pejorative?*
- No. Not from their viewpoint. Moreover, I prefer the term 'instrument' to that of 'channel'. An instrument transmits information more precisely than that which can be conveyed through a simple channel.

Feeling stiffness in my legs, I stood to limber up with a few steps.

- *Was Ergozs here today?*
- *Oh, yes! He thought your ears were really beautiful!*
- What?

I related the conversation I'd had with my new friend from elsewhere, who, I was now certain, encompassed a soul. Though different to our own, it was just as precious, if not even more so!

6

A Danger More Dire Than Death!

Seated at a Montréal café across from E.K., I watched the last snowflakes of the frosty season waltzing on the breeze. The icy breath of that wintry wind only served to remind us that spring, still dormant under a cloak of white, was overdue in announcing its arrival, with the buds yet to form on grey branches. E.K. pursued his thoughts by way of explaining to me:

- Their energy source is thermal-based rather than through sound waves. Avgaard and Ergozs are beings of fire related to the central Sun.
- *All the same, when I observe them I detect neither flames nor fire.*
- The body you see is an illusion, an envelope meant to reassure your mind, which believes that all is expressed through form. In reality, they are able to erase this illusory form instantaneously and become 'fire'. Their essence is of a fire that does not exist in our solar system.

I stared into my cup of coffee. My mind felt constantly challenged by question after question, arriving one on the heels of another at an alarming rate. Which was the right one to choose?

– *What really happened during this session?*

– You don't know? E.K. queried in surprise.

– *No, but that's because Ergozs sometimes conceals the identities of the persons and places you visit. That way I remain more vigilant to what is happening in the invisible around you.*

– What do you mean?

– *At times, certain negative forces rove around in your surroundings. They want to interfere with your work and prevent us from entering into contact with beings from other dimensions.*

– I know, replied E.K. Their presence is of greater magnitude on evenings when there is a full moon, and in the following two days, when the moon shows its full face. Describe to me what you have observed of these beings.

– *They assume different aspects, different forms. At first sight, some appear to be sympathetic; I would even say that they appear attractive. However, their eyes invariably betray their true intentions.*

– Are they honorable?

– *I would qualify them more as 'bad'. Those who appear more inoffensive in aspect prove to be the stronger, more cunning ones. They are quick to mock us.*

– Is that why Ergozs sometimes gives you a nudge with his elbow?

– *Yes... and so does T.M., when I don't manage to detect the threat quickly enough.*

- What is the greatest danger facing me… death?
- No.
- Then what?
- *That of being absorbed into another dimension which would imprison you, a state rendering you unable to interfere with their work.*
- Interesting! Can you tell me more?
- *In such a space, you would be cut off from everything, especially from us. We would have to come up with the right ruse to be able to go and retrieve you, which would prove to be an extremely delicate operation. The guardians of these forbidden places are very clever, adopting multiple forms and personalities at will. Such a rescue mission would require minute preparation and would be flying into the face of terrifying dangers: the risks of madness or death for us, and the risk that you will be secreted to a place even more remote and protected. You would be paralyzed in an immense inter-dimensional prison. For us to find you, and even for you to escape, would almost certainly be tasks that are… well, next to impossible…*
- How do such prisons function?
- *They are erected by magnetic fields arising from a system located outside of Sirius and the Pleiades. These fields contain living particles whose mission is to actively maintain the prisons by continually injecting an energy that transforms the atmosphere. This energy modulates and transforms the imprisoned form, rendering it invisible to outside viewers. The form is thus paralyzed! Spirit in the form is aware of everything happening,*

> *but remains powerless, with all actions being neutralized and absorbed by the particles feeding on them. Finally, Spirit tires and stops emitting thought-forms directed at possible liberation, making the task for potential rescuers even more arduous.*

- So, I could remain imprisoned for several years, or even for several hundred years…
- *That can't be allowed to happen; I would never get over it!*
- Don't worry about such a thing, but be on your guard.

On E.K.'s last words we both lapsed into thoughtful silence. There are silences so charged with intense energy that it would be sacrilegious to interrupt them. This was one of them. The minutes ticked by, silent witnesses to the precious time accorded us, and to the huge responsibility of the project that weighed upon us. He nodded secretively to himself and continued.

- *Tell me about Avgaard: who is he, what does he do?*
- Space and time do not exist on his level of existence.
- *If there is neither space nor time, then it follows that he is ageless?*
- No. Avgaard is still subject to time, but in a different manner. We could say there is a space-time distortion between his system and ours. In his current form, in earth years Avgaard is several thousand years old, which makes him relatively young for his universe. Over there, a life's duration, in a specific form[⚹], is

---

[⚹] We cannot refer to an 'incarnation' per se, as he does not have a body of flesh.

around five to six thousand years. In terms of years accumulated since his creation, Avgaard is older than our planetary Logos.

– *How is that possible?*

– When we study dimensions and levels, you will understand. The laws ruling the universe differ according to the vibratory frequencies emitted, due to the energy transmitted by the particular dimension of the level where these beings evolve.

– *That's not so easy to understand!*

– I know. Set your mind aside and simply let energy work within you. You will feel a through line of comprehension that has nothing in common with logic. Logic is a prison you must escape from in order to gain access to a much more immense system of comprehension. Don't limit yourself! By trying to understand what cannot be rationally understood, you perturb your brain, which tries desperately to transmit, through its nervous system cells, data that cannot be adequately received.

– *I would so much like to understand…*

– It's more that you would like to reassure yourself by enclosing your thoughts and beliefs within the four walls of your reasoning mind. This is what usually restricts the totality of the data that you receive from the outside world. This is an entirely different matter when it comes to spirituality, as you are well aware. Now, we are at the dawn of a new era, an era which will open doors to dimensions known to our forefathers…

– *What forefathers are you talking about?*

– About T.M., Blavatsky, Maitreya, Jesus and even the Buddha. They could not have attained such a heightened level of consciousness without realizing that we share the Universe with beings who, like us, evolve, love and grow.

– *Did they know about the existence of extraterrestrials?*

– They knew pertinently that 'sentient beings' lived elsewhere in other systems and that, among these beings, were custodians of wisdom. T.M. has always discreetly collaborated with these beings. He consciously recognizes that Tibet is an energetic platform that permits entering into contact with them. Why do you think the Himalayas have exerted such a fascination on people? Have we not the impression that this mountain range contains mysteries that only a few sages have been able to pierce? It is undoubtedly no accident that certain great Masters reside there. What's more, every single individual presently living on this planet Earth originates from a system outside of our own.

– *What are you saying?*

– For example, you and I come from… elsewhere. We have chosen to live certain incarnations here in order to deepen our knowledge of the Universe. Our Spirits are not restricted to this system. Spirit likes to experience, explore and learn. When we will have completed our apprenticeship down here, which could still take a few more lifetimes, we will continue to perfect ourselves elsewhere.

- *So then, my origins arise from another system?*
- Yes, and your home, before your arrival on Earth, was located on Venus. You have no recollection of it, do you? However, I recall that we lived together for several lives. Life on Venus is very different, and is in a sense easier than life here. Its energy is more subtle, more harmonious than that found here on Earth. If we could really unravel our origins, we would unlock some huge surprises.

My mouth gaping open, I saw a smile take shape on his face. My stupefaction overjoyed him. Trying to regain a bit of a grip on myself, I gulped down some of my lukewarm coffee. I once lived on Venus! How was that possible?

- And that's not all… You lived somewhere else before you lived on Venus.
- *You're pulling my leg when you say that, aren't you?*
- I have never been more serious. Why don't we talk about something else now! Do you have any questions about the session we just finished?

I started… E.K. always knows how to find just the right words to summon me back to the reality of the present moment.

- *The form in which I see Avgaard, is that a disguise?*
- More like a camouflage. The immense collar he wears hides the lower part of his face, which is composed of a different substance than the rest of his form. This substance resembles a crystal that glimmers according to the thoughts he has for us.
- *Does he use telepathy when he talks to us?*

- Yes, it seems to be the easiest way for him at this time. Telepathy is a universal language. The thought emitted is received in the magnetic field rather than in the auric sphere of the person who...
- *Why in the magnetic rather than the auric? Aren't they the same thing?*
- No, all beings possess a magnetic field, but not necessarily an auric one.
- *Aren't all beings surrounded by an aura?*
- No, the more bodies are integrated, the less an auric presence prevails. However, the light remains, though uniform in intensity and colourless. It is not related any more to the emotions or thought-forms. The thought is therefore received by the energetic or magnetic field and then translated into language by the brain. This is a rapid and very efficient process.
- *Isn't there a risk that the brain might incorrectly translate certain received information?*
- Of course! The quality of the exchange relates to the initiatory level of each party, dependent upon the vibratory quality of the light emitted and perceived.
- *Basically then, the purity of the light determines the purity of the language?*
- Precisely. With those who share with him the same forms of expression, Ergozs only uses his mouth when he wants to express himself more warmly.

– *Interesting! So then, telepathy can seem more reserved than verbal communication, not as warm?*
– Effectively, telepathy often proves less warm. It cannot transmit that particular warmth that arises with the vibration of the vocal cords. Sound is vibratory, and it adds an appealing, more personal note, to a conversation.
– *Isn't a sound's vibration determined by our emotional body?*
– In part. Emotion adds warmth, but an element of the vibration emanates from other parts or bodies that characterize us. The warmth or vibration coming from the soul tinges the sound very differently.
– *If I understand correctly, the warm side of Ergozs doesn't necessarily depend on his emotional body?*
– He doesn't have an emotional body, at least not an emotional body similar to ours. Their body of expression plays on a certain range that can appear emotional to us, but in fact these are only vibrations created by mental activity. As we so well know how, they too know how to tell 'mind jokes'. The sense of humour does not arise from the emotional body: it is a product of the mental body that, reacting to a situation, makes the sensitive cords of the emotive body vibrate. The interpretation of events and language creates emotional vibration. Most of the time, this process operates unconsciously.
– *Like a reflex?*
– Exactly.

- *Didn't the emotional body come on the scene before the mental body?*

- They were created simultaneously. The mental body is powerful, even in its embryonic form. Sometimes, it has difficulty controlling the reactions of the emotional body. Nonetheless, it is still the instigator of the emotion produced.

- *A mother, the moment she first sets eyes on her baby, doesn't she feel love for him immediately?*

- No. A certain unconscious process kicks in and determines the bond she will form with the infant. A mental decision, to love her baby or not, will then be made.

- *When they find they are unable to truly love their babies, don't some mothers, without much success, try to draw on their reason to develop a bond with their babies?*

- 'Reason' is not the same as the mental. Reason results from intellectual and social programming, arising, in turn, from the notion of good and bad. It is 'not good' to not love one's baby. The woman thus tries to reason, which has no effect on the emotional body. The mind 'knows', thanks to a feeling body, why she cannot love her child, and it will do what is necessary to have this wish respected.

- *What do you mean by a feeling body?*

- The feeling body encompasses the mental body and the emotional body. It perceives data which it transmits to the mental body, which it in turn transmits to the emotional body. It takes into consideration karma, life lessons to be learned, and bonds to be formed between individuals, the level of evolution, etc.

– *Does Ergozs have a feeling body?*

– No.

– *No? What does he have then?*

– He has 'another thing' which we will discuss some other time.

– *Does the same hold true for the way he looks at others?*

– In a way. Avgaard does not see us through his eyes. He perceives our thoughts, which are then mechanically translated into 'images'. However, by integrating into me, he succeeds in seeing through my eyes. During this adjustment period, I must be free of thought. One single thought could impede his vision. Until the integration is perfect, I must remain 'empty'. He uses my brain to communicate with you by 'thinking' about what you say to him.

– *Why are Avgaard and Ergozs contacting us?*

– Their motivations go beyond anything we can conceive and are unrelated to anything we might refer to as compassion or universal love. They are on another level entirely, aligned with cosmic equilibrium. We are integral parts of a plan, and their task consists of permitting this plan to move forward. For Avgaard, making contact with my physical body represents a risk. However, in order to accelerate our evolution, and by the same token their own, his motivation is much stronger than any risks to be run.

– *When you are in close contact with Avgaard, your physical form becomes almost transparent. You appear to be on the edge of an abyss, ready to fall in at any moment.*

– What you saw or felt is an energy source that stimulates their progression. It prevents the stagnation of their Spirit and obliges them to remain vigilant at all times. From our point of view, they live on the edge of a precipice.

– *Does death exist in their system?*

– Yes, but it is experienced in a way totally different from our own. For them, death consists simply of removing their consciousness from a form that doesn't allow them to expand any further, and to displace it into another form more adapted to their needs.

– *Isn't that the way it is for us too?*

– For them, this act is accomplished consciously. The substitution of form takes place simultaneously. The birth process, as we know it, is thus unnecessary. The new form is mature and ready to commence its work immediately.

– *Do they remember their previous form?*

– They remember everything. These are exceptional beings, just as we are. We have much to learn from them, and they have much to learn from us. This exchange is a mutual sharing.

E.K. paused for a few moments. Outside, the snow had stopped falling and the sun's yellow rays inundated the café. This privileged moment bathed my consciousness in a sparkling energy. We are so much more than we think we are, and we all come from elsewhere! How incredible!

> – I think we've done enough talking for one day; you need to integrate all of this. Why don't we take in a movie?

> – *Now?*

> – Yes, maybe the new Star Trek is showing!

I burst out laughing. Science fiction films end up touching upon so many truths. They present a plausible future… or is that more like a probable past? Are we extraterrestrials forging wonderful ideas of extraterrestrials? It was impossible to answer that question for the moment, but… was it really necessary? Did its echo not become manifest a split second before the question was formulated? My lips arched involuntarily into a smile. Life was still fascinating, despite its little bumps.

I stood up and followed E.K.'s lead to the doors of the closest movie theatre. A little popcorn with a soft drink was just what I needed to bring my feet back down to Earth, or at least back to this planet!

7
Ponder Carefully!

Men, or especially their souls, must unite forces to allow for a better exchange between what they desire and what God wishes. Our existence, as humankind, is in essence complementary to divine forces.

As T.M. spoke I listened attentively to his remarks. Seated in a straight-backed chair, putting pen to paper with all due speed, I jotted down every word he uttered about *Conclave of the Cryptic 7*.

- *What do you mean to say by 'complementary to divine forces'?*
- *Quite simply that we contribute to God's efforts to know his creation in its most minute details, whether atomic, spatial or multidimensional.*
- *Are we an extension of God?*

T.M. smiled at this.

- *We are more than that.*

I raised a sceptical eyebrow, doubting what I had just heard.

- *What real link do you think you have with Him?*

Abashed, I had to admit to him that I'd never thought about it.

- Do you truly believe that He created us?
- *That's what I always believed.*
- Are you really sure of His existence?

I felt uncomfortable in my chair, which seemed to be sinking under my weight.

- *If God did not exist, how could I exist?*
- Your thought pleases me, and I appreciate its logic, though I can qualify it as a 'trap'. God surpasses all logic, and it will always be so. He cannot be studied, spied upon, or even less so, understood.
- *Why?*
- Because He does not exist.

Shocked, I squirmed in my chair. I must have misunderstood!

- *Did I just hear you say, 'He doesn't exist'?*

T.M. smiled at my incredulity.

- It is true that He does not exist, at least, not in the sense that you believe. God is simply a vibratory note, one without either sound or light. He is beyond all that.
- *How can that be? If God is a vibratory note, that implies He has a waveform, a sound, a colour?*
- In your vision, yes, but not from the divine point of view.
- *What do you mean to say by that?*
- In actual fact, you and I represent two atoms within His divine body. The atom that we are cannot

know anything else besides its own vibration or limitation.

– *Which supposes that we do not know or cannot know more of what we think we know?*

– Exactly.

– *Are we thus prisoners of our cognitive world?*

– In a sense. To learn more, we should renounce our level of existence to vibrate on a different frequency, alien to our own.

– *Does that require us to become dead to ourselves?*

– More than anything, we should die within ourselves, in order to allow for a radical transformation of our world of perceptions, painted as it is in the colours of our beliefs.

– *Is the process you describe painful?*

– We could say it is 'uncomfortable'. Any transmutation, this term being more apt for this type of transformation, is always agonizing to endure due to the resistance of the old form, which subtly combats the new form in the process of becoming. The cry of protest of certain atoms is sometimes impressive when there is a mutation in the being to which they belong. This cry is often what the master perceives when his disciple is in trouble. Depending upon the note heard he knows what action to undertake to reinforce his pupil.

– *Is this a collective cry arising from the atoms?*

— Yes, from all of the atoms. Even if he thinks himself alone, man has a multitude of atoms for company, evolving within.

— *Is he responsible for them?*

— Yes. Each atom represents a life with its own evolution. Through these changes in consciousness, a man transforms everything by provoking the evolution of his own atomic system.

— *In what manner can such a change of consciousness make atoms evolve?*

— Through the principle of light. Any conscious process creates a light value that affects the vibratory field for the atoms. These then prevail on a higher frequency.

— *Are we composed of the same atomic field from one life to the next?*

— After a fashion. All the atoms making up our body originate in the indestructible drop or germ-atom at the level of the heart *chakra*. This atom contains the memory of our previous lives, here and elsewhere, and stays with us from one life to the next. It is our most loyal friend, because it knows from whence we came and where we are going.

— *Does it know our future?*

— Yes. For it, the past, the future and the present all form a single whole. They form a unique essence through which our originating atom evolves.

— *And this collective cry, does it have any link to the individual's personality?*

– No. The source of malaise does not come from the personality, but from the germ-atom that suffers by not being able to make the adjustment to a new frequency. Man's personality, invaded by such a state of being, is absolutely unable to comprehend what is happening to him. It questions itself, seeking practical solutions that are nowhere to be found. The ego, for its part, reacts by provoking the fear of succumbing to madness. The existential crisis that affects an individual's cellular world affects his precarious equilibrium, and thus he feels his very existence to be threatened. The master perceives this discordant frequency in his pupil and tries to alleviate the climate of cellular tension preceding such a major transformation.

– *Does the master transfer this tension onto himself?*

– No, but he supports a part of it in order to allow the pupil to succeed with his inner transformation.

– *The work of a master is remarkably complex!*

– Yes, and it's high time for a change.

– *In what way?*

– In several ways. One of the principal ways is for each individual to assume responsibility for his own evolution. The individual must not depend on someone else. He must be autonomous, while nonetheless accepting guidance.

– *Isn't that something of a paradox?*

– No, reflect carefully and you will understand what I am saying.

T.M. lowered his searching gaze on me.

- Do you have any more questions?
- No, I need time to consider all this.

He smiled lightly.

- You think much too much, which can, at times, impede your spiritual progression. Your intellect tricks you by creating, within you, fictional obstacles whose sole aim is to retard your progress. Control your intellect and don't let it manipulate you any more. You have no idea of the task ahead. Your intellect must become your ally.
- *Your remarks are a real mystery to me. Didn't you just incite me to reflect?*
- You must learn to reflect correctly. The reflection must activate your curiosity, which, in turn, must mirror an intense desire to 'know' that which is not yet known, but which irrefutably must be known.

Without another word, T.M. left the room, leaving me perplexed and thoughtful. I must not reflect... I thought. No, rather I must reflect in the right way. How can I get there? I am going to go crazy if I don't stop thinking in circles... I'm certainly not thinking in the right way right now. God help me! But... God does not exist! I shook my head vigorously to clear away my racing thoughts, expelling a great sigh. I knew that by acting that way I would never get my ideas into any semblance of order, though at the moment it offered some relief.

I got up. It was time to go. A meeting was scheduled with E.K. in less than an hour. I put my intellect on hold, or at least I tried, and drove my car quickly to the Centre.

The sky overhead was magnificent! For that whole day it had been covered in a thick blanket of ashen grey, lending it an unworldly air. I would not have been the least surprised to see an elf dancing sprightly ahead of me on the sidewalk along the boulevard. I couldn't take my eyes off the scene overhead. The sun, a flamboyant red orb, beckoned to my suddenly smitten gaze, appearing like the gigantic eye of a god lording over us, watching even our slightest gestures. I quivered. The day's strange atmosphere clung to me. What, I wondered, would happen? The usual limits no longer applied. All that truly existed was an indescribable tension, throwing into a vibrant light the transmission wires of the system interlinking each and every entity on this planet. I distinctly saw them, repeatedly criss-crossing, carrying thoughts and information of all kinds. I don't know what might have lain hidden beyond those surrealistic images, but the magic of that moment fusing with my conception of self will forever remain engraved in my memory.

I parked my car and crossed the threshold into the building. The silence of the corridors only served to amplify my otherworldly state of being. I had the distinct impression that someone was spying on me. I quickly turned to look. There was no one! A sudden chill danced down my spine. I was sure that there were eyes there, watching me, observing every move I made. I hastened my stride.

Finally, I arrived and entered the sanctum of the Centre. E.K. was there, meditating. His presence reassured me. I breathed more freely and took a position close to him. I soon entered into a deep meditative state. I had received precise directions which I was to follow during the session soon to get underway. We were preparing to experience an extraordinary contact.

When I opened my eyes, E.K. was watching me, a smile on his lips.

- *Are you ready?*

- *Yes, I am!*

- *Very well then, let's begin!*

I rose to my feet and stepped over to him.

- *The Council of 7 insists you lie down for this session.*

E.K. lay down on the floor. I offered him a cushion for a pillow. The floor's hardness would serve to anchor him to the material world. My presence would offer him support and a reminder of the human world. While he turned his thoughts inwards, I sharpened my clairvoyance. I had to remain alert, as this invisible world swirling around us holds an uncommon appeal. Feeling its presence, I felt not the least bit reassured.

I sat very close to E.K., on his right. I awaited a certain inner sign that would set the process in motion. Minutes ticked by, long and interminable. His breathing deepened. He gradually slipped into his inner centre, from where it would be possible to join this Universe that beckoned to him.

T.M. incited me to begin. Immediately, I applied the directives I'd been given earlier: I pressed my fingers on E.K.'s third eye and throat. Instantly, his energetic circuit accelerated. Stunning images appeared, images defying any logic, unreeling at such vertiginous speed that I was thrown slightly aback, teetering off balance on my haunches. I re-focused myself and regained my original position, more alert than ever.

An energy surge raced through the etheric channels situated at the level of his head. I tried in vain to decipher what information they transmitted. Feeling slightly dizzy, my concentration wavered. I caught myself and renewed my watch. I had to stay vigilant! I breathed more deeply, concentrating even more, hoping that my inner strength would soon adapt to his power.

Finally, I was there! My God, what a display! Thousands upon thousands of geometric forms circulated in infinitesimal channels. I edged closer. T.M. whispered in my ear:

– The Universe has just taken him into its core. Be vigilant and observe!

I stared at one channel in particular, transmitting a peculiar writing, symbols forming a language unknown to our planetary sphere. I leaned closer to try to make it out more clearly.

– You're looking in the wrong direction!

Hearing T.M.'s warning, I jerked to attention, all the while trying to calm my racing heart.

– Scramble the writing and you will understand.

I made a mental effort to do so. It was a code! He was being injected with a coded message. *Why?* I asked. By way of a silent response, T.M. confided:

– So that you will be unable to read it. He alone must understand.

The web of channels containing the codes became more and more active, engorged with an energy accentuating their vitality. They formed a perfect contour around his head, dipping slightly as if by magnetic force around the region of his third eye.

Avgaard slipped closer to us and touched E.K.'s third eye, provoking a cough that ejected him from his body. He was greeted by fine lines of light, attracting him into a universe parallel to our own. Channels then became apparent throughout the room. E.K.'s energy roved in search of one that suited him.

E.K. touched one of these channels and a luminous form, one of an extraordinary blue colour, approached him. The face of this form reflected a tranquillity and softness that revealed an extremely high level of wisdom. Those large, dark eyes looked upon E.K. with an intensity rarely encountered in this world. I could detect neither fear, nor hate, nor any hint of impatience or anger, only an expansive calm, as if a crystalline lake on a summer's night had settled there.

This being lifted a hand to make a sign and E.K., in his physical form, did likewise. The luminous form expressed itself through gestures that E.K. repeated textually[⁂]. An unlikely dance of words commenced. Both quickly gained confidence in the expression of this language known only to them.

Their gestures became ever more rapid and expressive. Jerky gestures to convey an affirmation and harmonious ones to express mutual understanding. Unfolding before

---

[⁂] As these gestures expressed a conversation, the term 'textually' is used intentionally.

my very eyes, a conversation was taking place between two beings whose cosmic configurations differed, but whose energies were in essence similar. They were brothers, speaking the same language.

My gaze lingered on E.K. His face glowed radiantly, reminding me of a child's awe at the magic of Christmas Eve.

He smiled from time to time, nodded his head, and even stole discreet glances my way. I was there, close at hand, watching over him even as I bore silent witness to an exceptional scene.

Without warning, E.K. began to intone the 'OM RAM' *mantra*⁎ in a strong, rich voice. He punctuated his chant with precise, energetic gestures. The visitor listened to him and upheld his side of the conversation with gestures of matching precision.

I couldn't say for sure how long this conversation lasted, with my gaze fixed ceaselessly upon the strange and magnificent scene. Gradually, the conversation became less intense. E.K. looked upon his visitor with tenderness, knowing that the hour of departure drew near. The luminous form raised his hand in a gesture of farewell, bowed slightly and disappeared. E.K. saluted him in turn. He looked calm, resplendent even.

The atmosphere infusing the room attested to the remarkable event I had just witnessed. Everything seemed muted and fragile to me. E.K. slowly but surely returned to us. His eyes, of a deeper blue than usual, sparkled with steely highlights. His quiet strength enveloped the room with a perfume strangely evocative

---

⁎ A *mantra* is a combination of sacred words, formulas or basic sounds.

of cinnamon. This scent overwhelmed me. The magic of the moment still flitted through the space, imparting an extraordinary atmosphere.

We smiled at one another. E.K. slowly lifted his hand to touch mine.

- Do you feel good?
- *Yes, and you?*
- I have a headache, but otherwise I feel fine. Did you see him?
- Yes.
- He was really impressive... though he didn't impress me in the least!
- *Yea, well... he sure impressed me.*
- That's normal, every little thing impresses you!

E.K. underscored his reply with a conspiratorial wink. I burst out laughing, as he couldn't be more right.

- I'm hungry. What about you?
- *Definitely! I'm in the mood for a good plate of spaghetti.*
- Alright, let's go!

E.K. rose to his feet. He seemed to me taller than before. How was that possible? Surely, I deduced, my imagination was playing tricks.

- What are you thinking about?

Not daring to tell him the truth, I replied:

- *When it comes down to it, we spend a lot of time eating.*

— I agree with you. This ritual holds a secret I'll share with you over our meal.

Feeling content, I fell in step behind him as he led the way downstairs and out of the Centre. The sky had lost nothing of its former splendour. We walked sprightly. I had not the slightest doubt that our meal would be excellent!

8

Russian Dolls!

We chose a restaurant I'm particularly fond of on Montréal's South Shore. Upon our arrival the owners, who knew us well, ushered us to a table out of sight of prying eyes. Having ordered a double espresso and a martini, E.K. asked me for my impressions of the session that had just ended. Surprised, I first asked him the reason for ordering a short double espresso, as he usually takes his double espresso long.

- This double espresso is for you. It'll take care of your headache.
- *How did you know I have a headache? And what's a double espresso got to do with it?*
- Your eyes give your condition away, and an espresso will relieve a headache more quickly than two extra-strength pills.

On those words, E.K. took the cup that Victor placed before him and set it directly in front of me.

- Go ahead, give it a try!

Incredulous, I took a good draught of the searing-hot liquid.

- *Yikes! That's hot!*

> – Go ahead, drink it down quickly. You'll feel the effect almost immediately.

Right then and there, I did as I was told. To my great surprise, I felt the fog of the migraine lifting and my feeling of nausea diminished almost immediately.

> – You see, it works!

I couldn't help but smile, he already knew! Not losing an instant, he continued:

> – I would like you to check with Avgaard if he comes from the same planet as the personage of light whose acquaintance we just made.

> – *I'll do so as soon as I can.*

After my reply, I savoured the last sip of my espresso. E.K. continued quietly.

> – Did you notice that Ergozs seemed somewhat passive during this session?

> – *Yes, he seemed to hold back in the shadows. How would you explain such behaviour?*

> – I don't think Ergozs possesses a sufficiently powerful energy force to enable him to remain in close proximity to such a personage.

> – *What do you mean?*

> – His electromagnetic configuration cannot withstand certain high-vibratory frequencies.

> – *Whereas we can?*

> – Yes.

> – *How is that possible?*

– Our etheric bodies are very robust. Their function is to absorb and adjust the various energy fields which may come into contact with our circuits.

– *If I understand correctly, the etheric body works similarly to a magnetic force field receiving and transmitting data?*

– Correct.

– *Why is it so robust?*

– Because it has suffered greatly. The conditions of life here demand a great deal of strength and endurance, the effect of which is to perfect our various bodies. Now, you see, each of these bodies fulfils a specific function, in synch with those fulfilled by the others, to serve as even more effective tools in the service of our souls.

– *We resemble a system of Russian dolls, with each body containing another even more subtle one that is its perfect complement.*

– Precisely. I would appreciate it if you would discuss this session still further with T.M. Try to get some more information on exactly what he hopes we will accomplish.

As I nodded in agreement, Victor appeared at our table, our main dishes held elegantly aloft.

– Let's eat now and give our grey matter a rest.

But it wasn't long before E.K. broke the as yet half-formed silence to interrupt the embryonic beginnings of my thought process.

- Victor is a really great guy, don't you think?
- *That's exactly what I was just thinking! But, on another topic, does food really embody a mystery?*
- You'd like to know more of this 'mystery', wouldn't you?
- *Oh, yes!*
- For the time being, I can tell you that food puts us in touch with our soul.
- *In what way?*
- You have to find that out on your own. It's a secret that can only be revealed through experimentation. We have to change the way we look at food. Our health only depends on its quality to an infinitesimal degree.
- *What do you mean?*
- Our health derives for the most part from the vibratory purity food contains. For example, a bowl of white rice, energized with love and consciousness, will feed you more completely than a filet mignon cooked impatiently and unconsciously.
- *This vibratory purity that is transmitted to the body, does it have repercussions on the link we nurture with the soul?*
- You used the expression 'nurture' appropriately, don't you think? Do you see the link? Food is nurtured, just as we nurture the link with our soul. There is a parallel between the choice of foods and the choice of companions who share both your meals and your

spiritual progress. You are what you eat, in all senses of the word, even when it comes to spirituality.

– *That's really intriguing! I wasn't conscious of food's importance to such a degree. Is that why all of the world's religions make an offering of food?*

– Are you referring to the link with the soul?

– *Yes. Do we desire to become closer to the soul by making an offering of food?*

– In less advanced times, we hoped the soul would save us, without however, expecting to make actual contact with it. Now, man's desires have increased, and his offerings have taken a tangent that makes him more responsible for his personal evolution and his desire for union with the soul.

– *That supposes that he no longer offers himself to God, or to his soul, as was previously the case?*

– That's partly it. Sometimes you're a quick study.

E.K.'s tone, between mouthfuls, was teasing. He suggested we change the subject. Though somewhat disappointed, I acquiesced. I was exhausted, as was he. These sessions, apparently so harmless, had in fact a profound effect on our physical bodies. These contacts with unknown dimensions impregnated our energy fields with vibrations foreign to our cellular systems. To varying degrees, they altered what we perceived, an effect which we could nonetheless sense. The body's molecular rate accelerated, causing fatigue in the physical body that required readjustment. After a good night's sleep, everything was usually back to 'normal'. We would have undergone an interior transformation, without anything appearing on the surface, however.

We finished our meal and returned to our respective obligations. The road back seemed to me interminable. No thoughts appeared on the horizon, as my cerebral circuits were, for the time being, quite incapable of functioning.

No sooner had I arrived home than I slipped off into my room to meditate for a bit. I needed such moments of respite to recharge my 'etheric batteries'. I closed my eyes and breathed deeply, placing my hands over my heart, performing a *mudra*⸸ to activate the heart *chakra*. Silently, I recited the 'SO HAM' mantra. Quietude soon engulfed me and I drifted off into infinity.

> – The support of the Masters, as far as your work is concerned, is unequivocal.

I started. T.M.'s familiar voice rang in my ear like a prayer bell. I didn't expect his visit again so soon. Seeing my startled reaction, he smiled.

> – You are surprising. The quality of your circuits confers an exceptional rapidity to the information transfers I wish to make to you. However, even if you understand quickly, a part of you, which we could qualify as emotive, does not comprehend or should I say, does not adjust as rapidly as your mental body does. You suffer from this, as you are aware of and know that it slows our work.

> – *What can I do about it?*

> – Not much. This phenomenon you experience originates in the astral body, whose time needed for assimilation is longer. This body is slower, and

---

⸸ A mudra is a sacred gesture, generally formed with the hands or fingers.

digests less rapidly. It has difficulty setting aside ancient memories. Its slower speed sometimes pollutes the other bodies and, in a sense, retards evolution.

– *How can I avoid that? Can I circumvent it?*

– No, as this is still the most efficient means Spirit has discovered to enable man to preserve his humanity. That which characterizes man, as a man, is neither his physical nor his mental body, but solely his astral body, responsible for the 'human gene' carried by man on this planet. Remove this body and we are no longer human, and then we would become strangers to our own planet.

– *It's slowing us down!*

– So it would seem, but such is assuredly not the case. The emotional body's function is to lead us to God, although undeniably in a manner that entails more suffering, this path is nonetheless much more effective, and thus faster. By this very fact, the emotional body avoids some planetary incarnations where a semblance of astral life is lived. In this manner, this allows for certain forms of life, different from our own, to experience this emotive phenomenon, part and parcel of God's plan, in order for this experience to be more complete.

– *Is not God complete in and of Himself?*

– God has not experienced everything, we experiment for Him. However, we are neither an experience, nor a part of Him that He uses to learn about Himself. We are an infinitesimally small version of

Him, infinitely incomplete, but of his divine Essence. Such a fact is difficult to put into words. In short, we are from Him while also being Him, without however being part of Him. We maintain a certain distinction that qualifies us differently from His nature while remaining part of this nature, rather than part of Him. Man seems complex, but that which we qualify as 'God' is even more so in its simplicity.

– *We complicate everything, don't we?*

– Save for rare exceptions, I agree. Sometimes, the dark powers like to do this work of instilling confusion for us, especially when we try to free ourselves from it.

I now want to speak directly to you on a more personal note. The goal of your life is to serve. This objective will become increasingly clear to you, since you are now breaking free of the chains of your past as well as those of your future as you know and fear it.

– *What do you mean by 'breaking free of the chains of your future'?*

– The perception of the future is often an impediment to evolution, as it entails emotional discomforts that prevent any such progression. You have been led, right from early childhood, to have more effective control of your fears and emotions. We also know that your most profound desire is to see the positive side of everything, even in terms of this feminine body that was so upsetting to you at a certain time.

– *I always had the impression that a woman's astral body interfered with her spiritual development.*

> – Quite correct, but not at the level of evolution in which you now find yourself. Your feminine body can, to a certain degree, exercise a greater influence than that of a masculine body. The 'mother' aspect, which understands and supports, completes the warrior aspect that your soul has chosen as a life experience during its planetary incarnations. You are here to learn, and you are doing it well.

E.K. has undergone intense moments during which he has touched upon an aspect of the Truth at the heart of the Reality of superior worlds that remain as yet unexplored by humankind. He possesses a powerful body that we can make use of, but rest assured, we will do so with wisdom.

> – *These worlds you speak of, have you already explored them?*
>
> – Never going so far as he has gone. I am not as well trained as a psychic athlete in this area of exploration as he is. I am a good trainer, but I do not have the cellular potential to accomplish such missions.
>
> – *I don't understand. Nevertheless, you are more evolved than he is.*
>
> – Suffice it to say, in simple terms, that although I am more ancient than he, and in this sense more evolved, I have reached certain of these spheres without however exploring them in any depth. Several factors come into play when carrying out such missions. These factors relate directly to specific qualities of soul or Spirit, which some possess and others do not.
>
> – *Do I possess some of these qualities?*

- I can only tell you this: if you enter into these spheres at this time you will stay there, which would be most unfortunate. Upon your demise, which will no doubt be conscious, we will see.
- *So then, these worlds are linked to the world of death?*
- No, there is no link with that sphere of activity where the souls of the dead are to be found. These worlds are evolutionary plateaus where certain beings, who are more evolved, spend part of their existence. We will reach these worlds, through the course of our evolutionary process, in several thousand years. These beings of wisdom can communicate certain information, and channels, such as your master, have proven useful. Don't worry; one of the functions of your emotional body is to be his protector. Does that surprise you?
- Yes.
- At times this emotional body is a protection, as it responds differently to danger than do our other bodies. The psycho-etheric body reacts without however seeing the real effects of its reaction; the mental body sees, but its desire for experience pushes it to exceed its limits. The emotional body, for its part, protects.

   You look tired. Is this the case?
- Yes.
- The source of your actual fatigue is not physical in nature, but arises from your brain which has received a great deal of input that it tries to digest and understand, though it operates in straightforward 'receiving' mode. Learn to receive without reflection.

- *I'll try, though that's not easy for me.*

- We are aware of that. Your presence in the execution of this project is essential. You should have no doubt of that. Your vibratory frequency adapts perfectly to that of your master, making for a team that was chosen long ago. You must purge your lack of self-confidence immediately; take steps so that this transformation will occur this very day. Your vibratory superiority must show through clearly to allow you to become a perfect instrument. You are no longer the irresponsible warrior of bygone times. You have known Merlin...

- *Merlin, whom we associate with King Arthur?*

- Yes.

- *His story always intrigued me.*

- You have known him well and been a loyal servant. However, you abused certain of the powers that you acquired. Rest assured that this will not happen again. You learned a hard lesson in the incarnations that followed, I personally watched over your progress.

I smiled at that thought and all it implied.

- *So then, I have known you from such far-off times?*

- Even longer than you could imagine.

- *What can I say? What can I even think about all of this?*

- Simply have confidence and do not complicate that which is easy to understand. Do you have any other questions concerning the project at hand?

- *Yes, is E.K.'s health at risk?*

– Are you referring to his fatigue and headaches?

– Yes.

– E.K. is currently undergoing a chemical and vibratory modification of his frequency and molecular composition. This is arising from his involvement with this project as well as his recent contact with this being, a contact that modified part of his internal composition. But rest assured, he is not in any danger. He is simply fulfilling his work.

– *What do you mean by 'chemical modification'?*

– From the molecular point of view, his atoms are experiencing an acceleration that gives rise to an effect on his consciousness. He cannot be stricken with madness or die. The faintness he feels, which causes him temporary discomfort, does not arise from the organs of his digestive tract, as you believed, but from the frequency that has been newly injected into his brain.

– *Is that dangerous?*

– No. The molecules are of a certain frequency that, when there is an injection of a luminosity superior to what was previously conveyed, demands a profound readjustment of the inner and outer vision. He is not 'losing something', but is in fact 'gaining something'.

– *This seems like a planetary initiation. Each one of them creates a greater and greater light within the individual.*

– Until he becomes pure light and perfect?

– *Yes, that's what our books teach us.*

— Your master reached this state quite some time ago. The process I am telling you about is something different.

— *In what way?*

— The light that has affected him since you started work on this project possesses a nature, and therefore a frequency, different from that which is injected during planetary initiations.

— *Are the effects somewhat similar?*

— No, there is a vague resemblance, but only when seen from the outside. The effects and consequences prove totally different however. Certain segments of the brain will change, which implies that the neurons will lengthen and thicken in order to permit the use of a larger area of the brain.

— *These neurons are alive then?*

— Yes, and in order to minimize the cerebral effort, they can distend during consciousness expansion.

— *The brain heightens its efficiency.*

— Basically, while receiving better and more abundantly, it transforms itself into a willing tool for the transfer of information.

— *How so?*

— The neurons transmit a greater abundance of energy to the cells of the brain, which in turn store more light and oxygen. This has the effect of increasing their efficiency, both from the point of view of nourishment to increase longevity and rapidity, and for the retention of more elevated vibratory concepts.

— *That's fascinating!*

— I know. What you thought possible only in the near future is actually accessible right now. We are no longer in 'science-fiction mode'. If each of you accesses your potential, you will become conscious and join as partners in a work that is not merely galactic but inter-dimensional, although when it comes down to it they are essentially the same.

The Knowledge is available; you must learn to reap its benefits as you would pick a ripe fruit. We will guide you!

T.M. bowed slightly, palms together as always, and disappeared. I was now alone in the room, which appeared to me much larger than previously. Suddenly, the road ahead looked like a long and arduous one. There was so much to be done, so much to think about, so much to change, so much to transmute... I cast a last look around the expanse of the room, which was nonetheless so familiar to me.

T.M.'s perfume still wafted through every square inch of this space that he had visited only a few minutes earlier. I breathed in this very particular scent, hoping by doing so to infuse myself with even more of this presence so dear to me. I rose to my feet and pulled the door closed with a soft click behind me... leaving the room as if it was the sanctuary for a precious stone, one from Tibet... one which would shimmer brilliantly forever.

9

A Mudraic Conversation

E.K. had telephoned me the afternoon before, wanting to know whether we could get together the next day to meet for our session. I agreed immediately... needing no time for deliberation. I was able to change my office schedule without any problems.

Driving towards the Centre, the wind buffeted my vehicle; its gusts forced me to clutch the steering wheel tightly. The atmosphere seemed charged with a malevolent energy, urging me to caution. I couldn't dispel the memory of the events that had occurred during my meditation of the previous evening. I felt such a tautness in the pit of my stomach that I wanted to throw up. I was eager to see E.K., and especially to see if he was alright.

I narrowly avoided a bird that wanted to get overly acquainted with my car's windshield. After that, I recited a mantra of protection and pressed on the gas pedal even more firmly. E.K. did not appear to be in any special danger, even so...

As if by magic, a parking spot freed up right in front of the Centre, allowing me to park and go in without delay. I wanted to walk briskly, but I couldn't seem to avoid tripping over every crack in the sidewalk. I was very eager to see him, to hear his voice...

I took the steps four at a time. Not very ladylike, I admit, but I couldn't care less. At last, I breathlessly reached the top landing. I tried to turn the door knob... and it wouldn't budge. He wasn't there yet! Disappointed, I consulted my watch: 10:00 am! We'd set our meeting for 10:15; all I could do was wait...

Seated on the doorstep, I concentrated on calming my hands, which, true to my spirit, trembled incessantly. I told myself that if I could succeed in calming them, perhaps I would have as much luck with my thoughts, busily spinning out of control in my head. The minutes dragged by, seemingly interminable...

Certain images, which I struggled to comprehend, surged from my memory time and again. The previous evening, during my meditation session, I had very clearly seen five malevolent entities roving around E.K. They moved ever so slowly... trying to penetrate his aura at the level of his heart *chakra*. Five treacherous forms with malicious expressions that still gave me the shivers! One crawled whereas the others floated in dark clouds, surrounding E.K. on all sides.

E.K. repelled their incessant attacks with difficulty, as they gave him no respite. I felt that his physical heart suffered some strain as a result. Powerless, I called upon the Hierarchy of the Masters of the Great White Way for assistance. Without hesitation, I clutched the book, *The Divine Concordance of Light*[⁺], an effective tool to emit invocatory vibrations in order to erect a protective shield

---

[⁺] *The Divine Concordance of Light - A Handbook from Heaven to Progression Earth* - Etbonan Karta, Orange Palm and Magnificent Magus Publications, Montréal, 2001.

to ward off the virulent attacks he endured. Over the course of the succeeding hour, I continually recited invocations until I felt a hushed stillness settle over the battle being waged in his small Montréal apartment. I didn't dare disturb him. What if all that had merely been the fruits of my overly fertile imagination?

That was the previous evening. Now I still sat waiting, becoming increasingly impatient. He was late in coming... which I found ever more worrisome since I couldn't help reminding myself: he is never late!

I stared at the floor, where my feet quivered fretfully. I had never before noticed the fine film of dust resting so serenely on the stairs. A good sweeping would do them a world of good, as it would for me, I decided and immediately set about it. It is odd that I find this simple act of cleaning so restful; letting me forget everything else and calm my spirit.

Finally, I heard footsteps on the stairs and rushed downstairs to greet him. He looked fragile and exhausted, almost vulnerable, most unlike his usual manner. He smiled weakly at me.

> – Excuse me; I'm not really feeling in any great shape today. It wouldn't have taken much for me to cancel our session.
>
> – *I know. You were attacked yesterday evening...*
>
> – Yesterday evening, and a good part of the night too. I still don't know how I managed to get out of it. There were five of them assailing me constantly; and so full of hate!
>
> – *I saw them.*

- Good! I hoped that would be the case. I transmitted you messages, warning you to be on guard so that you could confirm what was happening before your mind's eye. If possible, can you ask T.M. for more details about this attack? This is the first time I've had to combat such powerful beings.
- *I'll do so first thing this evening. Are you feeling strong enough to work?*
- Yes, just give me a few moments to catch my breath.

We entered the Centre, which always holds for me all the sanctity of a temple. Such a sense of peace reigns there!

- *If you don't mind, I'd like to meditate for a few minutes before we begin our new session.*
- I'll do likewise. I have the distinct impression that this session will be an extremely important one.
- *Are you alluding to the attack you had to repel yesterday evening?*
- Yes. I think these beings came with the express purpose of discouraging me, intending to prevent us from continuing with our work.
- *I had the same impression.*
- We will have to be careful.

Seated facing one another in the lotus position, we took a few moments to interiorize. A sense of calm washed over me and I felt ready to get to work. By mutual agreement, we settled in and readied to embark on our latest adventure.

My eyes riveted on E.K., I scrutinized the ethers surrounding him. No sooner had his eyelids shut than I saw some twenty personages encircling him. On the lookout for the slightest danger, I sat bolt upright in my chair.

– Don't be worried, these are guardians.

I jumped. Whose voice had I just heard coming from my right? I looked and then sighed with relief, seeing that Ergozs was there, close by my side.

– These are guardian representatives from the various other worlds. They will be on guard for your protection, as well as helping maintain equilibrium for this mutual exchange.

My eyes remained riveted on these beings as I listened to Ergozs. Dressed in long, brown-hooded togas, they wore white masks symbolizing the realm of death. They were also cloaked in silence.

– *Why do they wear such masks?*

– These masks serve to impede access to certain sites related to the realm of death. They also protect those who abandon the world of form prematurely.

– *Those who commit suicide?*

– What is 'commit suicide'?

– *You don't know?*

– These words hold no meaning for us.

– *That is an act by which we ourselves take our own lives.*

– You can carry out such an act?

- *Yes, we can.*
- *What strange people you are! One of us would never think of taking his own life; we do not have this power. Where we come from, life is sacred, and committing such an act would not be permitted to us.*
- We're not allowed to carry out such an act either.
- *And you ignore this interdiction?*
- Yes, though this gives us heavy karma to deal with.
- *What do you mean by karma?*
- That we have to pay for such a failure in a future incarnation.
- *Ah...! Now I understand why your lives are so short.*
- *What do you mean?*
- *Victims of your own ignorance, you do not have sufficient wisdom to act according to the Consciousness of your Spirit.*
- We know. It is so hard to annihilate ignorance!
- *You can never annihilate ignorance; you must understand and master it. Thus, it will change aspect and transform itself into your friend. Ignorance and Consciousness go hand in hand; never forget it.*

All the while, I watched E.K. closely. His form blurred, and then he left his body to voyage to other planes.

- *Is everything alright?*

E.K. nodded in the affirmative and murmured softly:

- There are so many of them... Everything is going so fast!

He smiled, and then began engaging in a 'mudraic' conversation, akin to a dance. Doing so, he swept the air with graceful movements, thus conversing simultaneously with several entities at once. Then, without warning, he headed in another direction entirely, piercing through the various universes he visited like a rocket. I had a hard time keeping pace with his progress.

- I just saw the reptilian galactic world that our friend Luc hails from.

And so he travelled on, marvelling at his myriad discoveries along the way.

- His current resemblance is striking! We can even easily identify the epoch he lived here. Truly fascinating!

Then once again he resumed his travels at the speed of light.

- This speed is intolerable; it makes me feel nauseous.
- *Where are you going?*
- Ssshh! Watch and concentrate!

I took more and more notes, thinking I would never be able to transcribe them all. I felt dizzy and my fingers were cramped. I wondered how I would ever be able to re-read my annotations, as by then I was more scribbling than writing.

T.M. whispered in my ear:

> – Later, I will tell you what is happening at this moment. Note down every detail and allow yourself to be led.

E.K. suddenly interrupted his voyage; in preparation to become the expressive vehicle for Avgaard, who was approaching him. What a magnificent spectacle that was! I saw, in a transparent form, Avgaard envelop E.K.'s body, and then reach a perfect symbiosis.

> – Do you have a question?

I edged closer and murmured in the affirmative.

> – *Yes, I do.*
>
> – Ask your question.
>
> – *Speak to us about the soul's suffering.*
>
> – The suffering of the soul arises from the separation existing between it and its counterpart, which it considers to be its veritable Self. The soul must harmonize that which is found above and below it. It represents the point of equilibrium upon which tranquility of being depends.
>
> – *Does it serve as an intermediary between 'above' and 'below'?*
>
> – From your viewpoint, we would answer in the affirmative; from our own, in the negative.
>
> – *What do you mean?*
>
> – 'Intermediary' subtly implies that for you a separation exists. This schism is, in reality, found in your

brain, which constantly plays with a planetary state implying the dichotomy between good and bad, black and white, and so on.

– *Doesn't this condition prevail in your system as well?*

– Absolutely not. We live in the unity of all that vibrates and exists.

– *Then, dark forces do not exist in your system?*

– That is correct. However, the moment we exit the system, we must recognize the fact that involute forces, negative to your way of thinking, provoke the evolution of certain species in the universe to which you belong.

– *Can these be compared to catalysers?*

– Not at all, as they shade all they touch with the aim of taking over completely. Rather, we would say these are perturbing agents, which, though necessary in certain systems, possess an exceedingly dangerous potential.

– *In what way?*

– They can destroy the system in which they evolve.

– *Why allow them to exist then?*

– Because they accelerate rates of consciousness-raising, refine intuition and fortify the wholeness of being. Do you understand?

– Yes.

– Do you want us to continue with the topic of the soul's suffering?

- *By all means.*
- We would therefore say that the soul is divided between what it is as an egotistic being, thus an entity linked to an ego which serves as a tool to advance its learning on this planet, and the monad that is situated above it. Its work, or if you prefer, its mission, is to become the point of equilibrium between these two worlds that qualify it. All suffering is due to the resistance to what the monad, through the soul, wishes to impose on the form.
- *That is to say, on 'us'?*
- Yes. All pain is the psyche's reaction to the being that refuses, through its personality, to adapt to the superior desires of the monad which you sometimes, in your ignorance, associate with God.
- *The monad is part of God and in no way represents God Himself?*
- Effectively. Suffering and resistance are the tools of those who embark on the path of discovery to illuminate the real reason as to why they have been destined to come to work in the spheres of this, their own planet. Suffering is not an enemy. The more the form mounts a resistance to the process of imposition of the monadic will, the more the emotional body responds by feeling such disturbances and often, unbeknownst to consciousness, the more man's destiny leads towards the vision of his individual acquaintance with God. Do you grasp what I am trying to express?

- *I am not really sure.*

- Give it some thought; I can't tell you any more. You have received enough information and energy for today. Good-bye!

On that, Avgaard gave me a slight nod and departed from E.K.'s body.

- Is it finished?

- *Yes, Avgaard has gone.*

- I feel as flat as a pancake and just as cooked. I ache all over, my stomach aches and above all I feel nauseous.

I smiled, happy to hear him speak. His skin tone gradually regained some of the usual ruddiness of his cheeks, losing the milky whiteness he'd had. He was coming back to life, and so I could relax and breathe more freely.

- *This session was exhausting.*

- For you too?

- *I feel like I've expended every last ounce of my energy.*

- Give me a few moments, and then we'll talk about it.

E.K. closed his eyes and slipped into a secondary state, neither sleep nor wake. His body needed to recuperate. I rose and left the room, taking refuge in an adjoining room. Upon easing into an armchair, I closed my eyes and hoped to meditate to try to understand what had just occurred. I entered into a state of deep concentration and...

10

The Guardians of the 7 Temples

I fell asleep! Bewildered upon waking, I tried to open my eyes but couldn't. My eyelids felt as heavy as lead! I felt peculiar, even somewhat dizzy. I tried yet again to pry my eyes open, it was a lost cause. When I raised my right hand to my face and used my fingertips to feel my eyelids, I was horrified to detect they were as swollen as golf balls!

My heart racing and my eyes mere slits, I hurried to find a mirror, blindly bumping a low table with a statue of a meditating Buddha in passing. Automatically, I excused myself and stumbled forward, doing my best to avoid the various obstacles strewn the length of the hallway leading to the washroom.

The fear of confronting my face in the mirror tormented me. All the same, I had to... My arms outstretched to feel my way, my hands found the mirror and I drew my face as close to it as possible, knowing that rectangular object would reveal the bald truth in its reflection with the plain pitilessness of the inanimate. I drew in a deep breath and delicately found my eyelid openings with my fingertips: I eased them open and looked... in shock! The sight was awful, worse than I thought possible. My eyelids were swollen to such a degree they were almost transparent. Involuntarily, I backed away, trying to reorganize my thoughts.

It was hard to believe. I repeated my gesture and looked again: seeing the same pallid face with two disgracefully huge protuberances masking a look of horror at the image thus confronted. What was I to do?

I had no idea where E.K. might be. I desperately wanted to put on a better face before he saw me! I held a wad of paper towels soaked in cold water to my eyelids and recited a mantra with the hope it might calm me. I summoned all the inner strength I could muster, doing my best not to panic.

The minutes ticked by like hours. A tumult of possible scenarios fought for dominance in my head, heightening the malaise I felt surging in the pit of my stomach. Was this the result of some sudden allergy? How long would I stay this way? I especially wanted to avoid being taken to the hospital...

– Where are you?

Oh, no, it was E.K.! Looking for me...

– Are you alright?

– *Sure, sure... I'm fine!*

– You don't sound fine. Where are you?

I couldn't resist the temptation to exclaim:

– *In the washroom!*

– Are you sick?

– *No. I'm just having some problems with my eyes.*

- What kind of problems?
- *My eyelids are so swollen that I can't see a thing.*
- Open this door. Let me see what's happening.

His hand rattled the doorknob. In a mere matter of moments, I knew he would encounter my new physiognomy… I wished I was a hundred miles away. In a caring tone that stirred me still further, he implored me to open the door and show him my eyes. I obeyed. No sooner was the door open than E.K. burst out laughing, disconcerting me to no end.

- You certainly wouldn't make the cover of Vogue today! Where did you go off to, coming back with such a violent reaction?
- *I don't know. I woke up this way.*
- So you slept, then?
- *No doubt about it.*
- For how long?
- *I have no idea. What time is it?*
- Four on the dot.
- *How is that possible? I slept for three hours then, because I dozed off at around one.*
- Were you really asleep, or did you go… elsewhere?
- *You mean, to another dimension?*
- Yes, to another dimension.
- *I couldn't say.*

> – You should try to recall and meditate on what happened. Come here, I'll help you.

Standing behind me, E.K. cupped his hands over my eyes. I sensed heat penetrating my eyelids as a pleasant tingling sensation surged over my face. I could feel the swelling going down and gradually I was able to open my eyes. What a relief!

I diffused the energy concentrated in this part of your face. I won't be able to disperse all of it today. I get the impression you must have had some interesting encounters… I would like you to check if any other marks appear elsewhere on your body.

> – *Right now?*

> – Yes, before they have a chance to disappear…

Upon that, he left me alone. Marks on my body somewhere? I strongly doubted I'd find any, but because E.K. insisted, I took his advice and checked. I still had trouble seeing clearly… Oh, my God! What's that? Near my navel, I found a round swelling, and then I found another on my left hip. Finally, upon close examination, I detected a total of four swellings on my abdomen. It proved impossible for me to see if there were more elsewhere. With bashful modesty, I tugged my sweater back on and asked E.K. to come look.

> – I was sure you would find others. Is it okay if I examine your back?

> – *Yes…*

Gently raising my sweater, he informed me that three huge reddish swellings graced the middle of my back.

> – They look like stings! You have seven distinct marks on your body. Our friends have surely injected you with some substance while you slept.

I could hardly believe it was possible. I hadn't felt a thing.

> – Don't worry, they are our friends. Let's go get a coffee.

> – *In this condition?*

> – Why not? We'll find someplace discreet and discuss the events that have just transpired.

I felt listless, but I knew a coffee would do me a world of good. We eased our way outside and down to the street. The sidewalks stunned me with their brilliance. I had the impression I could discern every single point of light on the objects we encountered. As for E.K., he disappeared by my side in his own aura of brilliant light. What an odd couple we formed for those who knew how to 'see'. He, a golden orb of light, and myself, a body of flesh and bone with eyes like a frog! This Universe is certainly home to an odd collection of beings…

That evening I sought out my meditation cushion and tried to take refuge in quiet contemplation, forcing myself to forget the chain of events that had unfolded throughout the day. I emptied my head of thought, at last succeeding in attaining a state of silence and oblivion…

> – You passed the test.

Though his voice startled me, I recognized the particular approach T.M. chose to herald his arrival.

> – *What test was that?*

He beamed, sharing a smile I had rarely glimpsed from him. It made him look at least ten years younger.

- The seven marks left on your body were caused by seven sceptres varying in their energy and configurations.
- *I thought that you had used needles to inject me with something.*
- The tips of these sceptres are slender enough to create that impression. We have not injected you with any substances, but rather with energies that have altered your etheric body, marring your physical body in the process. In principle, nothing should have been detectable. Your high sensitivity proved us wrong; hence we will exercise greater care the next time.
- *There will be a next time?*
- Certainly! There has to be a next time. We want you to be more effective, receptive and resilient.

I didn't dare reply. He knew I had confidence in him, though at times I feel somewhat unsettled within the limits of this confidence. Where was he leading us with all this?

- I know that you would like more complete information about the twenty guardians that manifested their presence during the last session. All I need to say is that we must be extremely discreet. This information can only be partially divulged. However, we are allowed to say that they are the guardians of temples situated light years away from our planet. These temples represent dimensions to which we are intimately linked.

I smiled at hearing a Tibetan express himself in such terms. I wanted to pinch myself to confirm the quality of my state of awareness: was I sleeping soundly, or was I…

- No, you're not dreaming. Don't waste this precious time with such futile musings. Listen, and then you can ponder the situation later if you feel the need to.

Ashamed, I offered him my apology and…

- There's no need to apologize. However, as I was saying, we are closely linked to them and entering these temples calls for extreme vigilance.

- *Why is that?*

- Because there is a risk of provoking a destabilization that could have grave consequences on our evolution. Seven temples were contacted during this last session. E.K. visited several worlds at various stages of evolution, but most importantly, these worlds manifest themselves very differently. Some of these worlds are minuscule and could be contained in an apple, yet others take on gigantic proportions that could encompass several universes.

- *What you're saying amazes me!*

- I know; but you'll get over it. The degree of evolution is in no way qualified by the size of things, but by the chosen degree of manifestation. The universes are vast, and their exploration is of great importance, however, establishing contact with them is of even greater importance. During our last session, a relation was formed with the system some qualify as the 'Black Moon'; for there the sun reflects without any reflection.

– *What do you mean to say?*

– The light transmitted is of an indigo colour, as are the beings living there. They have no veritable form, at least, no form at all akin to our own. They learn to live consciously, with various elements composing this indigo energy that takes on a more implosive than explosive quality, and with their reflective glow on the inside.

– *Interesting... but complicated...*

– Much simpler than it might appear. The second temple E.K. visited relates to a planet whose predominant colour is green. There, entities of a lizard-like form live and evolve.

– *Can they, as things now stand, inhabit our planet?*

– We are in fact now playing host to beings coming from that far corner of the Universe. What's more, several races that wish to evolve more rapidly seek to dwell in our midst. On their planet, they learn to develop their intuition through the pathway of the mental body. They live for several hundred years and die of psychic illnesses caused by the aging of their cells, which are then no longer able to receive and process the information transmitted.

– *That sounds like a form of Alzheimer's.*

– Exactly. But unlike those afflicted with that disease on Earth, they expire as quickly as the flame of a spent candle. Nevertheless, their demise is thus swifter and less agonizing to endure for their entourage. A third, smaller system was also visited: this is a home to beings, related in colour to violet, of an incomparable purity. Their planet is smaller than a plum.

– *Is it more evolved than Earth?*

– Ten times more so.

– *What do they learn there?*

– Inter-dimensional travel. They evolve according to a modus operandi that encompasses a purely atomic consciousness. They prove to be 'atomic' as much in essence as in their growth. They do not expire before the completion of a cycle that persists for several millennia.

– *Is there a relation between evolution and lifespan?*

– They are directly proportional: the more evolved beings are, the longer and more intense their existence proves to be.

– *A lot of work remains to be done here.*

– Yes, but don't forget that current life conditions are very difficult, wearing out our human existence more rapidly. Therefore, you cannot wholly apply this rule to our planet.

– *Are we the exception to the rule?*

– We could refer to ourselves that way. Now let's talk about a different system that is home to immense beings, who seek to maintain the intellectual and akashic chronicle of the memories of the people and beings populating our system: they are the guardians. The fact that they do not belong to our system amplifies their effectiveness.

– *E.K. really contacted all these systems during that session?*

– In effect. That's why the session was so intense.

– *And so exhausting.*

– Undoubtedly. The fifth system reached welcomes beings of an extraordinary gentleness who travel by thought and do not display any colour. Their survival depends entirely on a known substance.

– *What substance is that?*

– Let us say an etheric one, although its energetic quality is definitely superior to that found on our planet. This substance allows them to proceed in a universe where they evolve, not by the expansion of consciousness, but through its implosion. Artificial light affects their energy field, and in doing so scars their auric field. They generate their own light. Here, artificial light can heal us, but in their world, it transforms them into subtly diminished beings.

A sixth level was also visited. The beings found there are of a perfect beauty, which proves highly luminous. Intuitively superior to us, these beings have a fragile, delicate constitution. They move about by means of slight etheric movements.

– *Like those presented to us in the film,* The Abyss?

– Their movements are somewhat similar, though differing slightly in form. In any event, the beauty of their motion is markedly superior. The seventh temple visited, a component of the World of the Devas, belongs to a world of legend known to the entire galaxy.

— *Are you alluding to that of the angels?*

— They resemble angels, though their role is not the same. They rove through the Universe, helping the World of the Devas to fulfil their given mission.

— *Are they supervisors then?*

— They are the source of inspiration. These angelic beings are threatened by the thoughtlessness and lack of awareness found in human beings who do not respect either nature or other humans and their future. This type of behaviour pollutes the ethers.

— *Do these angelic beings have a role to fulfil in the maintenance of form?*

— Yes, inasmuch as this applies to the mineral and vegetal kingdoms.

Listening to T.M., the depth of his knowledge never ceases to amaze me.

— *Thank you!*

— For what?

— *For everything... but above all for your presence.*

T.M. does not appreciate compliments in the slightest, and though I am well aware of it, at times I can't restrain myself from offering them.

— You need rest. Meditate well... and sleep well.

He vanished without another word. I was disappointed, for I would have liked to continue our conversation. I stood up; I needed to contemplate what had been said for a while before meditating.

One question troubled me: why was T.M. involved in such a project? What was his aim? He always had a precise goal in everything he undertook. What meaning lay hidden in his involvement? Was it really T.M. or was I in contact with an impostor? Who could answer me?

– I can!

I spun on my heel. That familiar voice could only have belonged to one person... 'My God,' I thought, 'how is he involved in this project?'

11

Nobody on Earth is of Terrestrial Origin!

This project became an obsession for me, stirring me down to the very depths of my being. As it progressed, my preconceptions and beliefs shattered into splinters that flew off to the far reaches of the Universe.

Are we really beings possessed of such potential? Though I sometimes wondered, I became more and more convinced, for the meetings proved incontrovertibly real. They profoundly perturbed me, opening uncharted and unsuspected pathways to my unconscious. I discovered new truths that led to wiping my interior slate clean in order to yield to a burgeoning awareness, one from whence arose altered perspectives about who we are, what we believe ourselves to be and what we hope to become.

It was a Tuesday morning, and I was on the way to my office. I firmly clutched the steering wheel of my car, as if to grasp a tangible form in what had become my universe, now always verging on the topsy-turvy. My thoughts gravitated to E.K., who I hadn't seen for the past five days. I could envision Avgaard's face superimposing on his own, making for a surrealist portrait which would have stood up to one of Picasso's finest.

We had made our appointment for three o'clock. I was impatient to see him. It was another cold day but I felt wrapped in the warmth of well-being; I sensed our meeting would be special.

Upon arriving at the office, I meditated for half an hour before dedicating some time to the writing of this book, which by now was taking up a great deal of my time. I wondered at the reception it might receive. Who would believe the story that unfolded in these pages?

I forced myself to concentrate and dedicated a full two hours to my writing. Then I prepared the room for the coming session: lighting incense and a candle, dimming the lights, and meditating yet again to centre myself within rather than on myself. I knew I would have to be particularly alert, listening intently to whatever might transpire.

A memory suddenly emerged to the surface: my meeting with H.M.! I could envisage his luminous form, from which radiated such disconcerting beauty. I could once again hear him announcing that he was one of the 7; and yet again my knees felt rubbery with the shock of this realization.

- T.M. and I are members of this *Brotherhood of 7*, responsible for the project that involves both you and E.K.

Struck speechless, I had found myself unable to reply.

- We are pleased with your participation in this project.

Upon that, H.M. smiled lightly, and then continued...

- Would you like me to manifest myself in one of my non-terrestrial forms?

My knees began to play a jaunty imitation of a tune on castanets while I tried to remain clear-headed and valiant. Such an offer was impossible to turn down; I simply nodded my head slightly to signal the affirmative.

His face then changed aspect and grew longer: his head became oblong, his eyes immense, and his skin tone shaded to an intense blue. Stunned, I realized H.M. was a 'Blue' being! His force quadrupled, resulting in a momentary creaking of the floor to which my feet were glued. I was doing my best not to faint, however faced with that form, it was a struggle… but then I sensed it was not wholly unknown to me. Had I already seen him elsewhere in this same aspect? Or in other circumstances?

The energy he emitted proved so intense that I weakly asked him to regain his habitual form, which he did immediately. Relieved, I then breathed more easily.

— Do you have any questions?

A myriad of questions raced through my head, which one was I to choose? I decided to go straight for the most logical one:

— *What link unites the* Brotherhood of 7 *with the Hierarchy?*

— This Brotherhood does not arise from the planetary Hierarchy, though it directly involves the Logos.

— *The Logos?*

— Yes, he gave his permission for this project to be undertaken under T.M.'s supervision.

— *So then you're not the supervisor?*

— Not at all, I am already occupied with a multitude of tasks. I am collaborating on the project, as an advisor, and by participating in various meetings. It would be impossible for me to supervise all of them.

- *Is that one of T.M.'s principal functions?*
- Are you alluding to the supervision of this project?
- *Effectively.*
- No. He is also busy with other projects that are equally important.
- *Why are you involved in this particular project?*
- Mankind is on the verge of accepting the idea that other galaxies exist. Through this project, we are working towards preparing for this eventuality. Did you know that nobody on Earth is actually of terrestrial origin?
- *No, I wasn't aware of that.*
- Earth is composed of incarnated souls who lived on other planets. Earth is an artificial creation, a learning ground that is not 'home' to anyone.

Upon that, I held my breath, hoping the conversation could last forever.

- Tell me; didn't E.K. mention in his writings that we have always been divine beings, not human beings?

I jerked to attention in my chair: how could he know that?

- *Yes, he did mention that some time ago.*
- What do you think he meant by that statement?

I felt a sudden dizziness, everything was spinning so fast.

- *Who are we really?*
- It is of little importance for you to know that now. Appreciate this planet and this earthly body that sometimes seems such a crude instrument to you. Humans are evolved beings who accumulate knowledge and experience and who, having lived in other systems, have learned a great deal. They are travellers who are not afraid to take risks. They suffer, and they learn through such suffering.
- *Are we really evolved?*
- Man is evolved, but he sleeps: for some the Awakening is long in coming. The Awakening unleashes the memory of what man really is. His apprenticeship here becomes a precious tool for voyages to other dimensions and systems. I can even affirm that man is more highly evolved than angels.

Though taken aback, I managed to collect my thoughts enough to pursue my line of questioning.

- *How is that possible?*
- The angels have chosen to prevail upon a certain quality of energy that engenders little change or possible evolution.
- *What are you saying?*
- They have opted for stability, for comfort in their being. The range of their learning experiences thus proves limited, as do they. They do not know anything of matter or the laws that govern it; furthermore they have absolutely no interest or desire to delve

into such a manner of existence. Among them, those who decide to incarnate adopt the ways of celestial travellers and thus cease being celestial parasites.

Once again, I bolted upright, asking myself what he could possibly mean by calling them 'celestial parasites'.

– Angels serve a function. However, at times they can impede man's more evolved consciousness, or I should say more 'awakened consciousness'. They do not belong to this planet in any way, nor do we find them in various other systems. We can qualify this devic world as 'experience'. They were created not as 'souls' but as 'magnetic beings' already perfect in Spirit; for this they pay the price of sacrificing their own evolution, which cannot advance. Their role consists of assisting the transformation of consciousness for certain beings. They are only conscious within the bounds of their consciousness, but for all that, they are not ignorant. Every form of consciousness has its limit, and angels are no exception to this rule.

I noted down every detail of what he said, wanting more than anything to share it with E.K. as soon as possible. He would be able to tell me if these concepts were accurate or if I had simply been hallucinating.

– Man is an adventurer who loves to take risks and confront challenges. He knows that his transformation continues elsewhere, in his immortality. There is so much to learn, so much to live and experience… There exists an intergalactic or cosmic religion whose fundamental precepts share very little in common with the religions of this planet. These religions are a pale reflection of this way of being, which is based on an immense respect for each and every one.

– *This religion, it's not based on love?*

– No, because in several systems love does not exist, at least not in any way akin to the meaning you employ to qualify it. Earthly love is an invention or a pale reflection of this indefinable energy that binds the whole together. Here we call it 'love'; elsewhere it goes by another name. However, love as it is known and exists on Earth is necessary. It allows the self to exceed its limits, for ignoring the superficial self can, little by little, lead to an even more authentic forgetting of oneself, to become increasingly dedicated to the service of others and finding a truer form of love.

– *Now would you mind telling me what role E.K. plays in this project?*

With a light smile, H.M. signalled his willingness to continue.

– E.K. is a transmitter-receiver, a 'magnet' to attract these beings to us.

– *Towards what end?*

– These beings want, through his mediation, to approach us in order to collaborate more directly and more authentically, so as to achieve the universality of peoples from different galaxies.

– *Is that even possible?*

– Of course! This contact is primordial for man's evolution. E.K. has visited certain places and met with certain beings living elsewhere in other systems. He must now invite them to come among us.

– *Will there be contact on a physical level? Can we meet them tangibly?*

– This direct contact will occur later, though preparations are already underway in Japan.

– *In Japan?*

– Japan shelters several extraterrestrials.

– *What?*

– They live in physical bodies and experience terrestrial life.

– *Do the Japanese people know anything about this?*

– No. These extraterrestrials are very discreet, though they are easily recognizable if you know the signs betraying their origins.

– *Could you tell me what those are?*

– The only clue I can share with you is this: part of the answer to your question can be found in their eyes.

– *So then, in reality, some Japanese people are extraterrestrials?*

– Effectively.

– *Are they aware of it?*

– Some are, but some are not.

Nobody on Earth is of Terrestrial Origin!

– *How can they be unaware of it?*

– Because in evolutionary terms they are still young and the temptation to reveal their secret would be too great.

– *You mentioned that no human is of terrestrial origin; what difference is there between us and them?*

– The difference is found on the level of the essence. By accepting to incarnate ourselves on Earth, we have adopted the planet's essence. This essence vibrates in us; we are an integral part of the planet and of its evolution. This does not hold true for those beings who only adopt the human semblance of being from this planet. They think differently, act differently and have no sense of belonging to Earth, and even less so, no stake in participating in its evolution. They are ill at ease in this physical body; they all want to leave and return to their own universes as soon as possible. Have you ever given a thought to the strangeness of their comic books? Study this aspect and you will understand.

– *Will the extraterrestrials always stay in Japan or will they adventure elsewhere, to other continents?*

– Twenty or thirty years from now, highly evolved beings coming from other planets will make actual physical contact with us.

– *As is currently the case in Japan?*

– No. In Japan, everything is being done under the cloak of anonymity. This new exchange will occur by the clear light of day.

– *Will these beings be more highly evolved than those now living in Japan?*

– I will simply say that the extraterrestrials living in Japan are not exactly 'extra'-ordinary: they contribute a great deal in technological terms, but little on the human level. They still have an awful lot to learn from us, especially with regards to the consciousness of the heart.

– *Why do we still have to wait another twenty years?*

– Because the pettiness of world consciousness is poisonous for these beings; we must expand this consciousness and purify it of anything that can interfere with these future contacts.

– *What is our ultimate aim in trying to make contact with these beings?*

– Man must, so as to escape the world of matter, welcome these beings to his territory in order to allow man to surpass his limits and truly become an entity belonging to all galaxies.

– *That sounds like what was shown to us in the film, Star Wars…*

– There is a similarity, with the exception that no war must be started. We will align with worlds that have never known war, famine or misery. We will meet beings who no longer adopt a physical form, simply etheric or mental forms.

– *How will we see them?*

– The 'mediums' will see them in their true embodiments; others will see them due to the costume they will wear to protect themselves from the harsh and sometimes harmful effects of the material world.

– *That's really fascinating!*

– We hope that these explanations will encourage you to pursue this project despite the obstacles you encounter. Your friend is coming, give him my regards and work well!

With that H.M. bid his farewell and left the room, leaving a wisp of golden mist in his wake that soon dissipated. I turned to look out the window just in time to see E.K.'s car pulling into the parking lot of the building. Though slightly unsteady, I stood to greet him. Walking proved something of a problem, as I couldn't feel my feet. I was outside my physical self, and I knew I'd have to reintegrate rapidly. I drew in several deep breaths and shook myself all over, hoping to shake off the feeling and slip back into my body as if it were a glove that had momentarily gotten away from me. Luckily, it seemed to work, and I soon felt better.

I opened the door to E.K., who arrived with his arms laden with books.

– Hello, I found some books that should interest you.

I smiled broadly, glad to see him. As I watched him set the books down on my desk I thought to myself that I was very lucky to have met up with him in my little corner of the universe.

Was this really just a coincidence, or was it the fulfilment of destiny? Undoubtedly, I will never really know for sure, though when all is said and done, such certitude will matter little. Now what really mattered was that he was here, in this very room, and that we were getting ready to pursue the most wonderful project I had ever had the chance to participate in!

12

Our Future Lives Have Already Been Lived

L ook what I found!

E.K. took a book off the pile on my desk and opened it.

— Don't you think it looks like somebody we know?

A quick glance at the magnificent photograph he showed me confirmed his impression, revealing a Tibetan monk with a familiar profile, his eyes cast reflectively low... it was him! I took the book in my hands, seeking closer contact with this face that seemed to open a window to the mysteries of T.M. Was it him? I couldn't be sure it really was. I lifted my gaze to meet E.K.'s, murmuring:

— *Is it possible?*

— It appears so.

I couldn't believe it! My eyes devoured that photo, my fingers lightly caressing the image I encountered.

— If it's not the case, the resemblance is uncanny, don't you think?

— *Whether it's him or not, this is an extraordinary gift. I can feel his energy transmitted through this image.*

Upon my exclamation, E.K. drew closer. I could sense the depth of his gaze scrutinizing the face revealed in the portrait I cradled in my arms.

> – This photo serves as a catapult for him, his way of encouraging us. It allows him to transmit his protection and power to us when the need arises.

I smiled even more broadly; thinking that an extraordinary day lay ahead of us.

> – Are you ready for us to undertake a new session?

> – *Yes, I am.*

> – Very well then, give me a few minutes to meditate and then come join me.

E.K. went into the adjacent room and closed the door. For a few brief moments, I once again contemplated T.M.'s image before gently setting the book down on my desk. Our work was calling to me and I had no time to waste. I meditated for a few minutes and then prepared the things I would find useful during the upcoming session: pencils, a notebook and a tape recorder.

Some fifteen minutes ticked by before I slipped into the next room. I sat down facing E.K. and synchronized my breathing with his; attuned to the slightest of signs indicating that we could proceed. Then I saw Avgaard take a position behind him as Ergozs transposed a few metres from me.

> – The session can commence.

E.K.'s quiet intonation scarcely broke the silence, his eyes remained closed. I observed the total scene: E.K. entering into profound meditation; Avgaard watching for the precise correct instant to incorporate into him; and

Ergozs watching over all of us like a mother hen with her brood. I could sense that they were all very serious, even unusually so. In a moment of worry, it occurred to me that everyone seemed especially concerned. Ergozs watched E.K. more attentively than ever before. I could only wonder why?

His attitude intrigued me to such an extent that I sat bolt upright in my chair, alert to the invisible becoming more and more apparent before my very eyes. Avgaard gradually integrated and I saw them as 'one', even while simultaneously remaining 'two'.

I asked myself what was happening. Then Ergozs commanded me to remain calm, which proved a challenge I felt unwilling to accept. Upon his renewed insistence, I ultimately acquiesced.

I tucked myself deep into my chair, trying to unclench my jaw which had become as tight as an oyster refusing to yield. At the same precise moment, E.K. trembled all over, letting a moan escape. His brow taut, lips tight, he twisted in place, trying to resist an energy that gradually heightened his discomfort, he even appeared to be in pain. What could I do?

Ergozs chastened me to remain calm and observe closely. E.K.'s forehead broke out in tiny beads of sweat. Avgaard too looked discomfited in the position he shared with E.K.: he stirred as if he sought to remove himself, even as some invisible force held him prisoner in that body that was not his own.

Then they were no longer alone! Beings surrounded them; floating forms encircled them to create a wall of energy I could no longer penetrate. These personages murmured unintelligible sounds that only Avgaard seemed to comprehend. E.K. vacillated momentarily, and then quickly resumed his staunchly upright position. He gave the impression of waging battle with an invisible force just in order to remain in place, or maybe I should say, to stay alive before my very eyes.

If I'd had claws, I would have exposed them to their limit! A certain force seemed to glue me to my chair, though I felt ready to leap out of it at any instant. E.K. half opened his eyes and then shut them again immediately, murmuring:

– Don't worry, everything is alright.

Tears cascaded down my cheeks: he was asking the impossible of me! Once again, he gave me a brief look, the slightest of smiles forming on his lips...

– I'm alright.

The pain made him release an involuntary whimper, as if to contradict his declaration. I felt certain they were forcing him to submit to some test. What was it? Why? The minutes passed... interminably. I recited mantras interspersed with prayers. The stress twisted my solar plexus into knots, whereas the springs of my chair, despite my attempts to master them, threatened to expulse me at any moment. I had to calm down, it was imperative! Without letting my eyes wander from them for an instant, I started to count backwards to occupy my mind: 100, 99, 98... 45, 44, 4... I heard E.K. exclaim 'Ouf!' at the very same moment as Avgaard was ejected from his physical body.

E.K. opened his eyes. He looked exhausted.

– I couldn't hold on much longer!

He breathed rapidly, like an athlete at the end of his race. Avgaard looked at him, then saluted me and left the room, followed closely by Ergozs. I would even say they gave the distinct impression of fleeing the room.

> – *How are you doing?*
>
> – *I'm frozen...*

E.K.'s voice sounded weak, he rubbed his hands vigorously. Meeting his gaze, I could perceive part of him had remained behind in a space-time outside our own. I placed a blanket over his shivering body and turned up the thermostat. Then I rubbed his feet, which felt like blocks of ice through the woollen blanket.

His breathing gradually calmed down. I could see him coming back to life, his 'presence' slowly but surely illuminating his aspect.

> – *That was some journey!*
>
> – *Do you feel like talking about it?*
>
> – No, I'm exhausted. Let me sit here on my own for a few minutes, I need to recharge my energy.

I smiled broadly, happy for his 'return'. Then I left the room, quietly closing the door behind me. I wanted to meditate, hoping T.M. would be in the mood for a chat. I had so many questions... I felt my head would explode if I didn't get answers to some of the most tormenting ones!

I settled into my armchair and... I fell asleep! I remained in that state for more than half an hour, awakening only when I felt an invisible hand tugging my right earlobe. I started in my chair, doing my best to calm my racing heart, which seemed ready to leap out of my chest from one beat to the next.

– Once again, you fell asleep.

T.M.'s bemused tone betrayed a hint of mockery. Trying to inject some semblance of order into my thoughts, I replied:

– *I don't know what happened...*

– Don't worry; there are more important things to discuss. Would you like me to review the session that took place today?

– *Yes.*

– You should know that it shut a door that will now remain locked forever.

– *What do you mean?*

– The light you observed comes from a subtle plane that we refer to as 'atmic'.

– *Is this level related to the soul?*

– In effect, E.K. has welded his soul and Spirit to his being. Therefore, there will be no possibility of future contamination by what we call the 'defects' of the human race. He passed a non-planetary initiation, one closely linked to the levels located above the soul, beyond Spirit, and above all, beyond this world.

– *Could you explain that further?*

– From out of the darkness of his humanity his cosmic consciousness has been forged. He is now recognized as one of us; a 'young' cosmic initiate. He has survived a test, an element of his destiny, which I could not prevent him from having to endure. Little by little, he will now gain acceptance as a traveler of galactic worlds.

I listened carefully, drinking in each and every word T.M. uttered.

— Though still young, he has enormous potential. The initiation he has just undergone has various components. Here are the three main ones: the mastery of temporal space; the mastery of dark and material worlds; and the perfect mastery of the vehicle of his soul.

— *Can you elaborate further along those lines?*

— Of course! Let's start with 'the mastery of temporal space'. This state indicates that E.K. is freed of the concept of time in space, as he is also freed of the concept of space in time.

— *I'm having trouble following you.*

— I know. You have yet to achieve this state of being, and he alone can truly grasp the hidden meaning behind my words.

— *Will I understand some day?*

— Yes, but not in this lifetime. Let us continue with 'the mastery of dark and material worlds'. This segment deals with the planet's law of gravity, as well as all the involuntary aspects that pertain to it, in order to allow the Spirit, by gaining access via the vehicle of the soul, to travel in between the physical atoms of various galactic systems. Do you understand?

I thought I detected a hint of teasing in T.M.'s last question, but in all honesty I could only reply:

– No, I don't.

– That's quite normal, for you have yet to reach this state in yourself.

– *And I won't reach it in my present lifetime?*

T.M. smiled indulgently.

– Effectively. You are quickly learning what you need to learn.

– *I'm trying.*

– Would you like to gain some insight into the third segment?

– *Definitely!*

– The third segment, which we call 'the perfect mastery of the vehicle of his soul', allows him, if he so wishes, to use his soul as a vehicle authorizing him to travel in other dimensions without fear of losing his way.

– *How is that possible?*

– His soul emits a particular note recognized by his Spirit. If the vehicle, the soul, seems lost, the Spirit, through the intermediary of his other subtle bodies, can retrieve it immediately.

– *The Spirit has its own bodies?*

– Yes, but can we talk of that some other time?

– *Why not now?*

- Your head is already full of information it is having difficulty assimilating. Divulging more data of this nature would only be a waste of my time and your energy.

- *I understand; so you were saying that the Spirit retrieves the soul should it get lost?*

- Exactly... when the Spirit has mastered the vehicle of the soul. The soul is firmly linked to the Spirit and can no longer ever be impounded, stolen or lost. This is an irrefutable, inescapable law.

- *Why is the soul used as a vehicle?*

- The soul represents a 'memory bank' necessary to the human condition. It reminds us who we are by evoking the memories that link us to this planet.

- *Is that necessary?*

- Yes, as long as we have a physical body, the soul remains an indispensable vehicle. It allows the human being who has become perfect to travel in other dimensions without ever forgetting the point of departure, which also serves as the point of return. Without the soul there would be no recollection.

- *Isn't our brain responsible for memory?*

- The brain retains the memory of superficial details: temperature, bank account number, address, and place of residence, for instance. It retains no recollection of essential facts: evolution, karma, good and bad, or past and future lives.

- *Does the soul recall future lives?*

- Yes, 'possible' future lives, for all has already been experienced by you or me.
- *Could you tell me more about that?*
- The future exists because the past is the wellspring of its existence. For there to be a past, there must be a future. This future determines the choices to make in the past, and by this fact, enables the stability of the present moment in all things.
- *If I understand correctly, the future determines the past as much as the present?*
- In a way. Humanity embodies a destiny whose realization, whether fast or slow by degrees, is influenced by the time factor.
- *Therefore, all has already been 'written'.*
- All has already been said, written and experienced.
- *Are we then simply the memory of God who remembers through us what has already been lived?*
- I will simply ask you to reflect further upon this conversation so that we may speak more of it some other day. The only clue I will give you now is this: do you not sometimes have an impression of déjà-vu when you live through certain events?
- *Yes. However, it is not God remembering, it is me.*
- Isn't that one and the same thing?

His answer provoked a complete sense of the void inside my head. I felt like a prisoner between two space-time continuums where nothing seemed to exist. Only E.K.'s voice brought me back to the present moment... the passing moment.

- Where were you? I called you three times, you didn't answer.
- *I was with T.M. We were speaking about God and the concept of space and time.*
- Did you ask him if we were a dream dreamt by God?
- *No, but he mentioned that we might be memories contained in his memory.*
- Very interesting. What more did he say?
- *That I must reflect further on it.*
- He's right.
- *What do you think?*
- Of the fact that we are memories?
- *Yes.*
- I'll reflect on it.

Upon that comment, E.K. laughed. As for me, I didn't know what to think.

- I can't do the exercise of reflection for you. When you find your answer we will talk more about it.
- *Will I find the answer?*
- How can you doubt it? We all find the answers to our questions when the time and place is right.
- *Timing is so important then?*
- Yes, because it comes from the future...

I was stunned by his response, I could only wonder, how could he know?

– I can see, by your energy, that your physical body needs nourishment. What would you say to a good steak?

– *A steak we have already eaten in the future?*

– Yes. Do you remember the bottle of wine we had to go with it?

I couldn't help but laugh. Of course he was pulling my leg, but it was good to see him back to his old 'future' self.

– *No, not really!*

– Well, you need to practice then! Seeing the future is no more than reading what has already been lived.

– *Ouf! It'll never finish then!*

– What will never finish?

– *The revealing of what we really are.*

– That's right. Everything is only just beginning!

– *Will we learn who the "7" are?*

– Yes, very soon...

The night following this meeting was truly exceptional. The sky, perforated by the infinity of twinkling stars, seemed to observe us from on high. We perceived the presence of thousands of beings concealed behind that vast expanse of brilliant points. Beings who, like ourselves, wondered about life beyond their space. Of course, 'Everything is only just beginning!', but that particular night seemed to seal a common pact between us and them, a pact that would permit contact to continue.

 © Paume de Saint-Germain Publishing
Division of Orange Palm and Magnificent Magus Publications Inc.©
235 René Lévesque Boulevard East, Suite 310
Montréal, Québec, H2X 1N8, Canada
Telephone: (514) 255-8700
Facsimile: (514) 255-0478
E-mail: info@palmpublications.com
Web site: http://www.palmpublications.com

Imprimé au Canada par
Transcontinental Métrolitho